W9-CGR-092

Something in My Eye

SOMETHING IN MY EYE

stories

Michael Jeffrey Lee

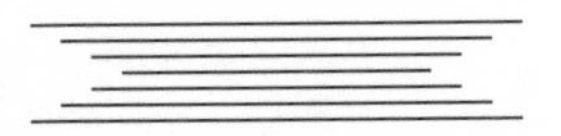

WINNER OF THE 2010 MARY MCCARTHY PRIZE IN SHORT FICTION

SELECTED BY FRANCINE PROSE

FIRST EDITION

Managing Editor
Sarabande Books, Inc.
2234 Dundee Road, Suite 200
Louisville, KY 40205

Library of Congress Cataloging-in-Publication Data

Lee, Michael J. (Michael Jeffrey)
Something in my eye : stories / Michael J. Lee.
p. cm.
ISBN 978-1-936747-05-4 (pbk. : alk. paper)
I. Title.
PS3612.E3455S66 2011
813'.6—dc23

2011025306

This is a work of fiction. Names, characters, places, and incidents either are the product of the author's imagination or are used fictitiously. Any resemblance to actual persons, living or dead, events, or locales is entirely coincidental.

Cover Image: Daniel Richter, "Jawohl und Gomorrah," 2001. Oil on canvas, 255.1 x 370.7 x 3.6 cm / 100 ½ x 146 x 1 ½ in. Courtesy Contemporary Fine Arts, Berlin. Photo by Jochen Littkemann, Berlin.

Cover and text design by Kirkby Gann Tittle.

Manufactured in Canada.
This book is printed on acid-free paper.

Sarabande Books is a nonprofit literary organization.

This project is supported in part by an award from the National Endowment for the Arts.

The Kentucky Arts Council, the state arts agency, supports Sarabande Books with state tax dollars and federal funding from the National Endowment for the Arts.

CONTENTS

Foreword

Three or four stories into Michael Jeffrey Lee's *Something in My Eye*—I believe it was right after I read the phrase "The motel had complimentary toilet paper"—that I became aware of feeling what I can only describe as a rush of gratitude, pure and simple. Specifically, I felt grateful that a press like Sarabande exists, so that this remarkable story collection will be able to go out in the world and find other grateful readers.

Mavis Gallant, who is among the very greatest short-story writers of this (or any) century, has said that stories should not be read one after another, but one at a time, with pauses in between. In the pauses between reading the stories in *Something in My Eye*—not *while* I was reading them, because they held my full attention—I had begun to imagine a conversation. This fantasy discussion seemed to be taking place between a literary editor at a mainstream publishing house, a real reader who admired the singular voice of a writer, let's say Michael Jeffrey Lee, and a person from the marketing department, who had a very different opinion. I kept hearing what the marketing person would say, the adjectives predicting why this book might have an especially difficult journey from the point of origin to the point of sale and into the hands of the consumer.

Here's how that side of the conversation might go: Too dark. Too strange. Too disturbing. Too many of the characters are not automatically sympathetic. You certainly don't want to date them or go out for a beer with them after yoga class or working out at the gym. Worse still, it's hard to find another book—another book that made money—that one can compare this to, another book that this collection more or less exactly resembles.

All of which is true, and all of which is why I so admire *Something in My Eye*. Of course I would eliminate the "too" in front of dark and strange and disturbing. The other objections—excessive originality and characters about whom we may have mixed feelings—are in my opinion major recommendations. I myself don't read to meet more people I'd want to date or have a beer with.

I was drawn to Michael Jeffrey Lee's lineup of loners and drifters, imperiled children, and haunted psychos neither because I want to hang out with these bad boys, nor because I plan to cross the street when I see them coming, but because the invitation to inhabit their minds, to see the world through their eyes, and to watch their often unsettling stories play out in space and time enables Lee to do all sorts of extremely interesting things with consciousness and language. If I failed to mention the marketing person's discomfort with the loopy off-key humor, perhaps it's because I wasn't sure if he or she would even register how funny these stories frequently are.

Allow me to quote from the passage that, for me, sealed the deal. It appears in the story "If We Should Ever Meet," which is narrated by a man who had been fired from his job for reasons unrelated to the private hell he's been inhabiting because he semi-lied about seeing a man jump from the roof of his office building. Even as our hero goes through the motions of moving to a new town and "starting over," he is haunted by memories of a brother who, before he was redeployed and killed in battle, used to lead the family in a "vague and kind of ominous" song he'd written about meeting strangers, a song which the family found "controversial" because they weren't strangers but close relations.

> In the mornings I would shower and shave with a disposable razor and soap, which was sometimes tricky because I tend to grow hair inconsistently, at inordinate speeds along different parts of my face. The motel had complimentary toilet paper, so I was able to staunch any of my cuts with little folded scraps before I left my room. One day though, I was in such a hurry that I cut myself under my nose, bad enough that I had to ask the manager nicely for a Band-Aid. People gave me nasty looks on the bus that morning, and I only figured out why, when, after I had filled out an application at a coffee shop and was using the bathroom in the back, I noticed that I had a pretty sizable amount of blood in my teeth, which I wasn't able to taste because of the cinnamon gum I was chewing. My brother's song went something like: *If we should ever meet, I will kindly take your hand. If we should ever meet, I will cudgel every lamb. If we should ever meet, I will wear my cleanest gown. If we should ever meet, I will set fire to this town. If we should ever meet, I will deny those close to me. If we should ever meet, I will feign to disagree.*

It's hard to explain precisely why I found this passage thrilling. Either you get it or you don't. But it did make me wonder why my imaginary person from marketing didn't seem to consider the existence and tastes of readers like myself, who are drawn a literary experience that sends one's brain on a sort of roller-coaster joy ride careening from sentence to sentence. I enjoy the suspense of not knowing where a phrase or a thought will end up, let alone an entire story. I like trusting that the destination to which I'll be taken will be rewarding, and that it won't be anywhere I would have thought to go on my own.

Another story, "The New Year," takes place on the bank of a river where an even further down-on-his luck narrator is living on a couch that literally fell off the back of a truck and over the side of a bridge in the course of a catastrophic auto wreck. As the story opens, our hero is bathing in the river and listing all the things he has to be thankful for.

1. The recent return of my health.
2. The range of my mobility.
3. The fact that there was always someone listening to my prayers.
4. The fact that I had not been murdered at any time the past year.
5. My couch.

At the end of the story the narrator explains why he has troubled us with this narrative that involves (among other things) his odd manner of life, a meeting with a stranger, a suicide, and what may strike us as a uniquely dada approach to political campaigning. "I want to end this positively . . . because I know that these kinds of moments are the only things people remember from the stories that they hear. I want to leave you feeling good. But however you feel, good or bad, for some reason, right now, I feel the need to tell you that, selfish as it might seem, the most important reason why I am telling this is because I want you to remember me."

Reading the stories in *Something in My Eye*, you will want to tell this character and his creator: Don't worry. I do feel better. And I won't forget you.

—Francine Prose

Something in My Eye

Warning Sign

I was seated comfortably in a bright room, surrounded by cameras and microphones and the people who pointed them. On a table before me, just as I had requested, they had placed a glass of spring water and a plate of decadent cheeses. I had contacted every major news outlet I could find the day before, telling them—should they offer enough money—that I would consent to a taped interview on the subject of the perpetrator. Normally I would have tried to abstain from capitalizing on an atrocity, but I was unemployed at the time, and a bit frustrated with the direction my life had recently taken, and so, after considering the exorbitant sums that they offered, and imagining all the ways in which the money would help me get back on track, I decided that it would be an act of incredible pride to turn them down, and so complied.

"It's hard to believe that only twenty-four hours have passed since the incident," they said.

"Yes," I said, "when I close my eyes, all I see are the faces of the dead and missing." This was true. I had found it difficult to sleep the night before.

"It will haunt us all for many years to come," they offered.

"It?" I said.

"The event yesterday," they said.

"Something new will replace it," I said. I ate a piece of cheese.

"Tell us how you knew Buddy."

"Buddy was my roommate."

"We understand that you and Buddy had other roommates. . . ."

"Oh yes," I said. "But they lived in different parts of the house. Have you spoken to them?"

"They've agreed to talk," they said, "but you're our first, among those who knew him. We were told you knew him best."

"I knew him fairly well," I said. "We had different schedules."

"So you shared a room with Buddy?"

"Yes," I said. "Our beds were on opposite sides of the room, next to our desks."

"Was it your decision to arrange the room this way?"

"I suppose. I guess that it was."

"Did you see Buddy yesterday morning?"

"Do you mean the morning of the atrocity?" I asked.

"It will be difficult for us to continue this interview if the word 'atrocity' is repeatedly used. Many of us have friends who have friends who have friends who perished in the . . . yesterday."

"I'll try to work around it," I said.

"You seem a bit detached, given the trauma of the last twenty-four hours."

"My grief and anger are packed so tightly inside me," I said, "they might take a few minutes to loosen themselves."

"Take us through yesterday morning."

"Well," I said, "when I opened my eyes from sleep, Buddy was performing jumping jacks in the middle of the room. He liked to do them very slowly. He would raise his pale arms and clap them together. He was very steady. Are you familiar with the paleness of his skin?"

"It is very pale," they said. "What else did you perceive?"

"Sometimes, during his jumping jacks, his hands wouldn't meet each other and his wrists would slap together."

"There seems something symbolic in that action," they said. "A circle closing, then reopening. The hands slapping against each other, eager for something to do. The very hands that would later that day. . . . How did you fail to pick up on it?"

"I suppose you have a point," I said, "but I focused on the beauty of his movements, nothing more. Is that acceptable? I feel as if I'm on the witness stand." I was trying to stretch the interview as long as possible, because several of them had offered to pay me by the minute instead of a single lump sum. At this point in our conversation, beneath the table on which my water and cheese lay, I had uncapped my pen and begun scribbling on the palm of my hand.

"Please don't get upset," they said. "If we sometimes sound harsh and insensitive, it's only because we aim to find out the truth of yesterday morning."

"I'm doing fine," I said.

"And besides, appreciation of beauty doesn't really pertain much to Buddy's story," they said. "There was, in fact, nothing beautiful about his actions yesterday."

"I'm aware of that."

"Are you also aware that at the jailhouse where they are holding him, he routinely asks—on the hour—to be executed?"

"Such a strange man," I said. "Out of curiosity, what manner of execution is he requesting?"

"A hanging. He has stressed several times that it must be public."

"It's not so good to hang a man," I said, feeling a little bold. "The rope leaves a hideous bruise. And the soiled trousers. . . ."

"So you are intimately familiar with the hanged?"

"Oh, yes," I said. "My brother went the way of the rope a long time ago." Again I was not lying.

"That's very sad. Very interesting and sad." I saw several of them dab handkerchiefs at their eyes. "Does suicide run in your family?"

"Oh, no," I said. "My brother committed an atrocity and was justly punished for it."

"How is it," they said, "that you have managed to avoid this kind of fate yourself? You carry your parents' genes, after all."

"I was adopted," I said. Also true. "I did not meet the people who made me."

"Here it seems appropriate," they said, "to ask how you came to know Buddy?"

"I answered his want ad for a roommate."

"Do you remember what the ad said?"

"Oh, yes. 'Happy man needs like creature to sleep on other side of bedroom and pay half the rent, until the day when roommate is no longer present among the willing, at which point remaining roommate will pay rent in totality or find other roommate.' "

"So you might admit that right away, the warning signs were there?"

"I find people very difficult to read," I said. "And I admired his honesty in saying that there would come a day when he'd be gone. I can't tell you how many roommates of mine have skipped out without any notice."

"Do you plan to search for a replacement, now that Buddy is gone?"

"No," I admitted. "I think a part of me still believes he will come back. I plan to leave his bed the way he left it."

"And what way was that?"

"Messy," I said, which had everyone, including myself, laughing for a moment.

Then a door on the side of the room opened, and several more of them walked in, carrying cameras and microphones. Some very good-looking ones approached me, and—whispering in my ear—offered outrageous sums for the chance to record the remainder of my interview. Obviously I agreed. I even signed the contracts with my own pen.

"Now," they said, "Did you two have a conversation while he performed his jumping jacks?"

"No," I said. "I knew enough not to disturb him when he exercised. However, when he was finished, he came and sat at the edge of my bed and leaned over me."

"The memory must be chilling now, considering what he was doing only hours later."

"I thought it was nice of him to devote time out of his busy day to me. While I pretended to sleep, he whispered a song in my ear. To interrupt him would have been a sin, his voice was so gorgeous."

"Tell us the nature of the song," they said.

"Well," I said, "the melody was rather rudimentary, almost folksy. Were it not for the lyrics, it could have been a children's song. He sang, 'Farewell endless toiling, farewell old shambling frame. I'm attending to my second self, reacquiring my good name. Please regard me joyfully, as you listen to me sing. I have an appointment in America, for to kiss the king's fat ring.' Then he went on to rhyme 'atrocity' with 'paucity,' which I thought especially clever."

"And how did you interpret those lines?"

"I didn't," I said. "I thought it was a spiritual."

"Do you realize," they said, "that he was spelling out exactly what he was going to do later that day? The fatalism in those farewells? The second self? The fat ring of the king? It couldn't be more obvious."

"Well, now that you mention it, his words do seem a bit prophetic. Maybe Buddy was trying to warm me, in his own way. He was quite a man." My heart ached a little for him just then.

"Did you say warn, or warm?"

"I don't remember," I said.

"In what way was he quite a man?"

"Well," I said, "yesterday morning, after his jumping jacks and that apparently clue-ridden song, I opened my eyes just as he began disrobing. He stood there, in his glory, for several minutes, until I told him to get in the shower or risk getting me a little hot under the comforter. I'm sure you know how well-proportioned Buddy is—you have access to medical records, correct?"

"Yes, but this is news to us that the two of you had a relationship."

"Oh, not at all," I said. "We were perfect platonic roommates. Only it had been a good number of months since I'd had a chance to ravish someone, so I was definitely ready to go. I'm sure everyone here can relate."

The room went silent. I looked down to see what I had written on my palm, but discovered that my pen had exploded—my hands were smeared all over with ink and nothing legible remained.

"We are," they said, "so deeply saddened by the . . . events yesterday, that it seems impossible, at this moment, to either empathize or fail to be offended by your sentiment."

"May I ask a favor?"

"You may."

"I'm feeling a little tickle in my lungs as I talk, and if it isn't too much to ask, I'd like a towel to expel the culprit into."

Then the door opened and one of them left. We all sat in silence. Some cried silently, shifting the cameras away from me and onto themselves, while into the cameras they mouthed the word "why?" over and over. Then the door opened again, and someone in white entered, making his way down the aisle. He placed the towel on the table. With a clean finger I drew it to the table's edge, picked it up, coughed several times into it, and then, when it was safely in my lap, used it to clean the ink.

"Better?" they said.

"I think so," I said.

"Though it pains us to ask this," they said, "you became aroused by Buddy's display?"

"That would be putting it lightly."

"And though it perhaps breaches matters of good taste," they said, "did you act on these feelings of arousal?"

"I touched myself beneath the covers after he entered the shower," I said, which was a lie. In truth, I had taken him in the shower, and he had cleaned every area unreachable to me. It was not the first time; we were practically strangers. It was just something we did once in a while.

"Do you value your life?" they asked.

"Certainly," I said. "I'd like to accomplish many things before I die. I'd like to see a solar eclipse or perhaps the northern lights, and/or hunt a grizzly. There are others, but I don't imagine you're interested in them."

"Does it worry you that, in light of these new revelations, you might be charged with aiding and abetting the perpetrator of this . . . ?"

"Those who charge me would be mistaken," I said, and I was being truthful again. "He clearly led a double life. It's not so rare. But let me just say this, atrocity aside: the Buddy I knew was smart, intelligent, playful, funny, mischievous, playful, easy-going, sensitive, playful, and considerate."

"What time did he exit the shower?"

"Nine-fifteen."

"What time did he leave the apartment?"

"Around ten-thirty."

"And the . . . , excuse us, was committed at eleven o' clock. Did you have any more interactions with him in the forty-five minutes after he left the shower and before he left the apartment?"

"Yes," I said. "He dressed, put on his backpack, and stood beside the breakfast table where I sat watching television."

"Do you remember what program you were watching?"

"It was the news."

"And what was being reported?"

"Something certainly paling in comparison to the atrocity," I said. Seeing that my use of the word really was affecting them, I just couldn't help myself anymore. "I apologize for using the word 'atrocity,'" I said.

"Try to remember. Maybe something he was watching set him off."

"They were reporting a story about a cat stuck in a tree. This happened in the ghetto, I think, and no fireman would try and save it because they feared the people who inhabited the ghetto. So for several days, and without the fire department's help, the ghetto-dwellers fed the cat by means of a long pole. 'And for the time being,' the reporter concluded, 'the cat is fat and happy on its perch.' The story was going to be continued the following day." This was a complete lie. I could not remember what I was actually watching.

"Did he say anything to you while you sat at the table?"

"Yes," I said. "Yes, right before he left, he stood over me and put his hand on my shoulder and said—"

But before I could begin, the door opened once again, and another one of them came in. He was dressed like the others—nicely, in a crisp suit—and he whispered in the ear of the person nearest to him. Then the person who received the initial message whispered in the ear of the one closest to him, and so on and so on until the entire room sat up very straight and began to fidget.

"We apologize for interrupting," they said, "but we have just received word that a lynch mob has broken into the jail and done unto Buddy what he has been clamoring for all day. Please continue, but do make it brief. We've lined up interviews with several mob members."

I was not ready, at that moment, to begin considering what all of it meant. Buddy was a fine acquaintance, but was he something more? It was difficult to know. We were roommates, and then we were not. I ate several pieces of cheese. I took a long swallow of water. I looked down at my lap, where my inky fingers clutched the inky towel. I looked out over the restless crowd. They seemed to require something more. So I took a deep breath and said, "He put his hand on my shoulder and said, 'Goodbye, dear roommate, I'm leaving this place, striking out for new country, settling the outer banks. Goodbye good roommate, I'll remember the long lost ribbon in your hair, playing gourd and hatchet in the gazebo long ago, oh roommate of mine. Though we didn't even know each other, didn't know each other's minds. It's such a shame, that we might have lived for so long together and been ignorant of each other. I am feeling so mournful, so solemn, sweet roommate. I want to believe in the future, but I can't see beyond my watch. I want to bite from the essence, the true root. I want to ride through the city in a caravan at dawn. I want the drums to encircle me, the vultures to wheel over me. I want the bitter bile of betrayal to flee from me. I want the warm expansive language of joy to radiate around me. Recall, oh roommate, that fine fellow down the hall who used to show his skin to anyone who'd cross their eyes. Recall that evening sun that set golden, golden, golden, then red in the west. Recall how we once shared this dim corporeal property together. Goodbye my sweet devil with flies in your eyes, you who saw everything as it should be instead of as it was. May there be some noble path shining somewhere for you; may the Lord keep a nice nasty watch over you. And to all my sweet darlings plunging from rooftops, to all my good ghosts forever ascending fearless: goodbye.' Then Buddy left for the atrocity." This was a bald lie, but it felt right somehow. As right as anything could, anyway, given the circumstances. Buddy had actually said nothing that morning, had really just abandoned me there at the table.

Contemporary Country Music: A Songbook

Title: SUPPORT THE TROOPS

Lyrics: could it be john walking though that door / at long last our son is home from the war we all still strongly support it is him isn't it / come give us a kiss and a hug all around / don't forget me john I'm your sister and I love you / did you see the banner we hung across the lawn the one that said welcome home john we are proud of you the whole state of alabama is proud of you / that uniform is as pristine as the day you left us john it sure is spiffy / I kind of expected it to be speckled with our enemies' blood john why not / oh of course they let you wash it I wasn't thinking john forgive me / what was it like over there all we had were our imaginations / we understand you don't have to talk about it if you don't want to but did you get the care packages we sent / your mother worked so hard on those packages john in fact it cost us a fortune to ship all that food even though I tried to explain to her that it wasn't as if there weren't grocery stores where you were there were grocery stores weren't there john / did you get the letters I sent john did you get all those letters from my classmates there were a lot of them / you must have been busy john but we were hoping you would write once in a while but I'm sure you were too busy defending and spreading freedom but none of that matters because you are home and the army can't legally force you to return for another tour and now you have some pocket money and college is waiting if that's what you still want to do / john wants to eat everyone gather around the table while we say a long and thankful prayer

Title: WE DON'T HAVE MUCH MONEY BUT WE HAVE A FAITH CALLED JESUS

Lyrics: before we all devour we have to give thanks to the man who is responsible for all of our business here who knows when you are sleeping and given to idleness and when you are supremely alert / we don't have much money never had much money / you could say that economic factors forced you into war but that would deny your individual choice dear john you understand you strong independent man son of mine / I guess you picked up the habit of not praying but just ask your sister she prays by her bedside every night and expects results so I don't think you can walk in here having forgotten all religion and expect us your dear family to understand when you deny the fact that jesus lord is upon you even when you least expect it / there are some principles which we all share surely you haven't forgotten the power of shared principles john you know you always carry the blood and beliefs of those who made you don't you john / I had a good day at school today yes we know honey but john is just freshly home from the war / here john have a piece of this steak you know how poor we are so it isn't everyday we eat steak but here take a piece of this and put it in your mouth it's tender isn't it / john likes that steak you can tell he likes it when he smiles that way / have another piece john you are too thin what did they feed you over there / you did not eat fear john is making a joke come on everyone laugh at john's joke / it's been a long time since we laughed in this house but we can laugh again with impunity because our boy the thing we made from scratch is here in the flesh and hungry

Title: THE WORLD IS FULL OF MANY PEOPLE THOUGH WE REMAIN PROUDLY IGNORANT OF WHAT THEY DO

Lyrics: yes john you can smoke in here your mother quit this year and I pretended to quit at least on account of your sister's asthma but go right ahead let me get the ashtray / something has been bothering us john now correct me if I'm wrong but your mother and I were thinking that the people you were trying to spread freedom to are people who don't actually want it and correct me if I'm wrong maybe I was born yesterday but I don't see how any person wouldn't want to be free we here in this country take it for granted but you can bet if someone wanted to step in and say no more freedom for you I would cut off his head and run for the hills where a man can still live free / I understand if you don't want to talk about it but it's just bewildering to me to think that there are certain people out there in this world who don't want what we have / all this is just to say that we know how tough the job must have been trying to give something to people who don't want it or maybe I have it all turned around I do all right john / well we can talk about this later right now is time for basking in your glory and not much else so I'll just drop the whole thing but I think we'll have to stay there a hundred years so these people will finally realize that they actually do want the thing they don't think they want right now let me have a drag of that don't tell your mother

Title: TECHNOLOGY IS OVERWHELMING BUT FUN

Lyrics: we could go sit in the family room and watch television together if you want to john / no you do what you want we're just happy to have our son home our hearts can begin beating again / yes we have a computer here john / but how are you really are you feeling well you don't look as good as we expected but granted we remember you as you were a year ago when your second deployment began but really we still imagine you as the same boy you were for your senior portrait come see it look at it we're still displaying it proudly on the mantel / you want to go on the computer rather than talk to your family well if that's your decision not one of us can stop you / yes we bought a computer we were influenced by all those advertisements which suggested that if we did not purchase a computer we would be dooming your sister forever because she would be retarded in terms of her peers what was I to do in the face of such an argument / yes just log in under the family name here it is / I didn't know you had a personal website that's very interesting john / why didn't you write if you had a page that was devoted to yourself and your life it would have been as easy as typing out a message and clicking the send button but I know you were busy with your business killing the enemy / mom and dad don't like the computer they feel that the second coming is nearby / I've never seen you so interested in something john I like it when you smile john it is wonderful to see your hands work overtime even at the computer which is a lonely pursuit

Title: DON'T FORGET ABOUT YOUR BUDDIES AT THE BAR

Lyrics: no john we realize that you need a place to go a man needs a place where he can kick back and unwind / where are you going well I suppose that really isn't any of our business but since we have you here since you are under our roof again we just want to know where you'll be so we can sleep better tonight of course your father will be up late drinking coffee and cleaning that rifle of his and thinking man thoughts but that's just what he does he is a man and a proud parent and jealous sometimes but a man's got to do / maybe he can come with you no all right john we understand you want to relax with your buddies or maybe you need to be alone hopefully there will be a band playing and you can have a few drinks / if you need a ride john call me I just got my learner's permit / take the ford yes john she still runs good she's american made after all / we are so proud of you you will never know the extent of our pride and our gratitude that god spared you out there in the desert he truly works in mysterious ways and I don't begin to understand his plan but your safe return all tells us that his plan is at the very least sympathetic to a family's fears / I know a lot of your buddies didn't make it and what about their families but still the point remains that you were spared for some purpose and so our faith remains as resolute as ever / have a good night john / goodbye john / I don't think many of us will get any sleep after all but you should unwind it's only fair I think you should relax a little you seem a little tense we love you

Title: EVERY MAN MAKES MISTAKES IN HIS LIFE AND AS LONG AS HE ACKNOWLEDGES THEM HE IS FORGIVEN

Lyrics: hey john welcome back you're looking good have a shot / have another its great to see you see that piece of ass over there what do you say we go hit her up for a little mano a mano / john tell us a story / the last time you were in here you'd just gotten back from your first tour and my god what a story how one night you lined a whole family up because you just knew deep down they were holding terrorists and you just lined all of them up and pretended that you were going to kill them but instead you fired a few shots in the air and then took them inside and gave all of them the old alabama slammer that was a good story honestly john because we all were thinking that it was going to end in bloodshed but you found a way to work off some steam another way and any time bloodshed can be diverted you've done a good job / you don't have to tell another story if you don't want to john but you know nobody's got loose lips around here we're all friends here have you listened to the band yet they're not bad they play here all the time why don't we just kick back here's another shot on the house relax and unwind I know that's what you came here to do

Title: OCCASIONALLY WE REQUIRE THAT OLD-TIME MOUNTAIN MUSIC

Lyrics: well john it isn't as if I can just kick the band off the stage just because you don't like what they're playing I mean it's what the people want look at them they're having a good time / it isn't people having a good time that makes you angry is it john I mean look at them they're drunk and happy and blowing off a little steam / everyone has to blow off a little steam once in a while you wouldn't disagree with that would you john / I realize you like the old-time sounds a little more than this contemporary stuff but listen for a moment they are singing songs about real people and their problems I mean maybe they gloss over some of the bigger issues at play I admit and it does seem that every other song they sing is about learning lessons which maybe you would disagree with because you never struck me as a lesson type of man but still / I know you came here tonight because you remember that we used to have an old-time band here on this night but you've been gone a year and we run a business john and nobody showed up for that old-time stuff so I'm sorry the band is almost done with its set hey did you get a look at that baby over there sitting all by herself I know you aren't exactly in as good a shape as you used to be but I'd bet good money she'd take you home that spiffy uniform holds a lot of clout around here you know

Title: HANG ONTO YOUR SMALL-TOWN VALUES WHEREVER YOU GO

Lyrics: nice to meet you john yes I love that uniform I was admiring it from across the bar I'm twenty-two you want me to guess your age well I don't think I should what if I get it wrong and guess too young and then offend your pride or what if I overshoot it and you feel like an old man no I'm not going to do that / no I'm not saying I oppose the war necessarily but I've been getting my degree at the community college and one of my professors well he brought up some issues that I wasn't aware of about the war no I'm proud of what you're doing as I said I support the troops / you should really think about giving college a try I'm not suggesting it would change your mind you haven't really told me what your opinions are I feel like I'm doing all the talking but think about college its been the best experience of my life my young life anyway I expect to have even better ones once I get out of this town / small towns are a little poisonous don't you think me I've always pictured myself in Nashville because I like the music so much that comes out of there no I don't know the old-time stuff as much as I should but I think I'd like it if I gave it a try do you have any recommendations / no well do you want to dance with me not sure well have a nice night and thank you again for all that you've done without you who knows I might not have even been alive to go to college the whole country might have been up in smoke though one never knows the indirect consequences of any action my professor told me that yes I'll leave you alone

Title: AS GRANTED BY THE CONSTITUTION EVERY CITIZEN HAS THE RIGHT TO BEAR ARMS

Lyrics: no john all the pawn shops are closed and wal-mart wouldn't sell you a gun with that beer on your breath no not even in that uniform I think you should just have a coke or something let me get you a coke at least the band went away I don't personally even like them but you can relax now that they're gone / I would john but I have to wake up early tomorrow no a long drive does sound good there's really nothing like a long nighttime drive to really blow off some steam but I think you've probably had too much to drink to really enjoy your drive and frankly I'd worry about your safety and with you just getting home and all / can I call your home who can I call who will be up / I woke everyone in your damn house up but your sister's coming to get you she's a good-looking girl / she's going to be a knockout in a year or so you watch you'll have to shadow her unless you want the boys climbing all over her but she's on the way now you just sit back and relax

Title: FOCUS ON THE FAMILY

Lyrics: oh john here help me get him in the car there you go john now sit back and relax I can't promise this will be the smoothest ride because I'm still learning what are you thinking about john / you don't have to tell me if you don't want to but I'm your sister and I want to know what's bothering you but if you don't want to talk I understand here just sit back I'll turn on the radio do you have a favorite station there's this song I want you to hear it's about a man who gets home from the war and cant make sense of his surroundings and I'm not suggesting that this has happened to you I think everything makes perfect sense to you but the man in the song has just come home and his wife has given birth to their child while he was overseas and so he's going around the town feeling sad which we all do sometimes even I get depressed it's only natural / so he's driving around and he gets so depressed that he thinks about maybe enlisting again because life was exciting over there and in another part he thinks about actually killing himself but he gets over that pretty quickly when he sees his wife rocking their child one night very tenderly and he has this moment when he realizes that god has put him on earth to be a good father and not dead or overseas and then the song ends / I don't want you to think though that this applies to you at all / for all I know you are planning on going back for another tour or you want to die but I just thought you might like the song because it had a soldier as the main character I think it feels good to hear those songs because they are about real life and music is so important because I think it shapes who we are and what we think and in the south especially music is even more important than most places the music reinforces our values I'm not suggesting that music is the only thing that helps make us what we are but I think it's important do you mind if I turn on the radio

Something in My Eye

Let me try to be clear: I'm sorry for leaving your side. Obviously, it's a bit late to make it up to you, so I don't really intend to try. Instead, I thought you might like an update on my progress.

I accepted the transfer, moved down south, and began my career in slaughterhouse management. The salary was competitive, and the company paid my moving expenses. It was the chance of a lifetime.

You should see the cows in the early morning, when they're bathed in the light that the sun sneaks onto the world. The scene is almost pretty enough to make me forget what's in store for them.

I recently received this message from a stranger: *What a lovely, lovely evening.* I called the person back, hoping to inherit some of that evening, but no one answered. Then I sat down and composed a short, stupid soliloquy: *Oh memory, I'm your unwilling creditor.* That's all. It's very short.

I have two squirrels in my backyard here. They leap and tumble together, death-defying all day long. But that isn't the worst part.

When they grow tired, they turn their black eyes my way to see if I've been watching.

This is a story I recently overheard: A boy, not so old but not quite young enough to be forgiven, gets himself lost in the woods. He's all alone, no one around, no helpful animals, the trees all shaking their heads incredulously. It's the afternoon, maybe dusk; it doesn't matter, the light will be back tomorrow anyway. The boy is tired; he is hungry, talking to himself, speaking a lovely, lost language. On the third day, he is found and returned to his family, who want nothing to do with him anymore.

Mostly I take stock here, at the slaughterhouse. That seems to be my main job. A missing tongue, a surplus of hooves. I try and keep track of these things.

My dead friend—you remember him—our dead friend once said: *Keep your chin up, that's all there is to it. Look at me, I'm keeping my chin up.* This was before he died, of course. You remember him. He grew rice as a hobby.

Summer here is a little difficult. Potentially desperate. On the street corners, boys wave their cardboard signs: FIVE DOLLARS WILL FILL YOU UP PIZZA. There's nothing I can say to them, passing them by, gone, except sometimes I hang an imaginary sign over my own eyes: BOYS I WOULD BUT I'M LOOKING FOR THAT EMPTY FEELING HAPPY SNARING.

I call my sister from time to time. She says to me: *Verily, verily, verily verily. You know I love you brother, verily.* I can't say it doesn't feel good to hear that once in a while.

The last time I saw my parents, they assumed I was dying. Or at least quickly disintegrating. My father, in a rare uproar, planted a kiss right on my mouth, hard, like he used to do to my mother, how I used to do to you. I never did make it back to see them before they died, which I regret. What was one more terrible kiss, if seeing their son brought them just a little bit of joy?

Lately, I've been doing something I call *running by.* I strap on my shoes, I pull on my shorts. I wear no shirt because of the heat, and because I'm not old enough to feel ashamed of my body. I sprint under street-lights, through redneck yards. And though I keep my eyes fixed in front of me, what I'm actually doing is honing my peripheral vision.

I wrote this on my mirror in lipstick yesterday, but don't think it applies to me or you or anything, really: *There once was a man who needed affection, badly. He wasn't so tall, a little on the mangy side. Always he walked downtown with his arms spread wide, in the hopes of an embrace. What an asshole; he died a violent death.*

You know, the only thing keeping me from death is the unsubstantiated feeling that it is worse than life. That was the only issue we ever disagreed on, I think.

I love hearing the wind whisper cryptically. This is what it said yesterday: *The price is paid. The price is paid every hour of every day.* I have yet to decode that particular one.

While driving, I saw gas prices change before my very eyes. A magic hand pushed four into five. I took slow, deep breaths, pulled over, and got myself into some air conditioning.

In a bar, I saw a songwriter sing her haunted guts out. I wrote this on a napkin while listening to her sing: *Human beings are not so cheap.* Then I put a date next to the entry, as if the moment was important. I must have been about eleven or twelve drinks in. Still easily duped, I'm afraid.

I shouldn't tell you this; it isn't very flattering. I spotted the Devil on my street, as I was returning home from work. He was easy to recognize. I spoke to him, asked him to turn around. When he finally faced me, he kept his hand in his pocket. I asked to see it, then blushed. I didn't really want to see it. I just hated the idea of him keeping things from me. The next night, he was on the front stairs. I could hear his light, perfect steps padding up to my door. I flung it open, knowing it was he, but I was too late to greet him—he'd gone hunting some other. I unlocked every door, every window. Later on, I heard him sliding dishes in the kitchen while I dreamed. I got out of bed, demanded, begged him to show his hand. Instead, he fooled with himself in his pocket until I went back to sleep. The next morning, I found him dead on my sofa. I picked up his hand. He had nothing to be ashamed of; it was just an ordinary hand. I tell you this only because I want you to know that the Devil is dead.

Sometimes I masturbate on my front porch. No one's around, the streets are usually empty, I'm no pervert. Just myself, my loving extension, and the ribald hissing of insects. I would stop, but it's never less than acceptable.

I came from a place of no history to a place where history has no place for me. It's my own fault, don't think I don't know that.

I was buying trifles one night at the gas station. A clerk asked me whether I'd ever heard a church bell toll. I told her no, feeling violated. Then I left. I was already in my car when I realized that she was probably just making conversation.

The man who bolts the cattle informed me that he was quitting. I told him his body was a galaxy, his eyes stars, some real low-down corn-pone to flatter him. I also complimented his detachment when killing. He asked that his last paycheck be sent home.

I nodded and smiled politely, but secretly, I was damning the distance of men.

I had a lover here. She was so good-hearted, too, so composed and calculated. One day, she found herself a bird that could talk, then set herself apart from me. Eventually, she lost the will to do anything but listen to the bird. I don't know where she lives now. But I did hear that the bird did not make it through the winter.

Not long ago, I took a vacation. I rode the train. Such a pretty, impoverished view I had. The soil recoiling from the broken buildings, the farm machinery all rusted out, the trees transfigured by their kudzu cloaks. Under an overpass, several afflicted but affable persons seated on a sofa enjoyed a cracked conversation. And later: a toilet, alone on a hill, patiently waiting to fulfill a purpose. And then, in a ditch, a man lying face down, his arms splayed in victory. That night, I dreamed what that dead man was thinking: *Wait, wait for me. I'm but an old, outraged thief.*

I often wake with my face turned to the sneering sun. This might surprise you, but it's usually easy for me to fall back asleep.

Some things to remember: Never call a lover while in disguise, never have a little something on the side, never hail from the country, never hail from the city, never hail ever, never move where they don't like you, never look for someone when they're already gone, never keep pretty dresses in your closet, for when you die, your relatives will raid your room and judge you.

I have something in my eye; I might as well go ahead and tell you. It's no bigger than a grain of sand, and does not impair my vision. It is aggravating, though. My doctor, may God grill him, suggested a risky procedure, told me that science had finally caught up with my problem. I agreed, signed the papers. I stipulated that if I was killed, they would have to bring me back to you and lay me by your side. He agreed, but the procedure was unsuccessful. That something was driven further in.

If I were ever given money to make a movie, I would get an actor, not tell him anything about the project, then fly him to the moon. I wouldn't pay him, wouldn't feed him any lines, I would just film him thinking.

Sadly, I've been driving drunk around town, floating through stop signs, taking generous turns. I reason it this way: either I'll go, or there'll be one less good old boy on the street. But sometimes I think that's too generous to them, and I'm only generous to those who worm their way into my heart. I was the one who wanted the plug pulled on you, after all.

You'd think that in my year here, I'd be able, just once, to catch a spider biting me. It's never happened. It's always the sweet patter of little legs, the vanishing act, the welt, the scratch, but never the moment of puncture. How do they do it?

I've been writing a number of essays on various subjects. Here's a small sample: In all my various travels through our great land, I have seen an extraordinary variety of dead things along the road. Most recently, I saw a vulture on its back, its claws curled toward the sky while the asphalt cooked him. The world would be a better place if I learned how to be like that vulture. I mean the finished product, the handsome corpse. The sign to the living: it isn't so bad. The end.

I can't prove this, but somewhere, here, in this town, outside a bar, there's a man in a bad panama hat and a wrinkled suit dancing with a friend, whose head is crowned with greasy curls. They sway and sway; under the streetlight they sway. The man removes his panama hat and suddenly releases his friend to the ground. I can't see blood from his head wound, but I can hear it trickling.

I had another lover; I'm sorry. She was an artist, in a way. She could have been famous in her time. She offered to draw my face for free. *An old face haunted by nothing,* she said. I told her I would like to live within her, but she told me that she had another. I told her I would be willing to live between her, her and her other. Then she said that loving me had grown her a conscience, and could I please leave her.

Here's an unfinished joke: have you ever woken up with your fist missing, only to find it on the end of your wrist again? As I said, it's unfinished.

All the cattle low until the final day, the one they can feel coming in their blood. Then they begin to moan. Isn't that terrible?

I would love to believe that God is both massive and passive. Did you ever make up your mind about that?

I might join the military. Maybe I need someone looking over my shoulder again, hunting me with my permission. I'll become a hard-liner, you know, spit in the eye of evil? Carry heads home in a sack?

Recently, I peered in the mirror, was surprised to see my smiling face. I decided that it couldn't be my face, that I must have acquired a new one during the night.

This is a beautiful story: when my mother died, they measured her brain and found that it had doubled its size. It wasn't even something she wished for; it was just given.

There are good woods near my house. They'll be gone next year, but for now, I can walk within them. At night, I walk within them and look up to the moon. I say, *Hey, you up there, drop a little silver tear down on me.*

I've been sleeping outside lately. I wake up covered in ants, with moths perched on my eyelids. They adore me out here.

You might like this town. There is just so much room for development.

My last fortune cookie: *If you don't believe us, raise the blinds.* I didn't eat the cookie.

The title of the children's book I am writing is "Where the Flames Reign."

This is me keeping my chin up, by the way.

I buy a lot of fancy ties. Not to wear. To run the silk through my fingers, between my legs. A nice tie is a nice tie, as far as I'm concerned.

Another lover, he was cold as a fish, but his skin was beautifully blue. He told me his love would change me, would prickle unknown zones. He fell asleep in my car one night and never woke up.

If all of history is held within the present, I don't think it's unfair to assume I will be failing the future.

I put an ad up for myself, selling my potential. Nothing fancy, just a picture of me in a jacket looking vaguely bored, threateningly curious.

It's only you I miss, you know. The people here don't do anything for me.

It's not that I don't agree with your decision to leave the world. This is not a judgment. At the same time, I do wish that you had finished the job.

I visited a psychologist only once. He tried to get me to remember a time when I was tickled as an altar boy. I told him there was no altar, and I was never a boy. Then I told him that people were meant to live bottled up, rubbed raw. Until the Great Ventilation, of course. On that day, it's our earned right to leak as we ascend.

I think I really knew what I was talking about then.

I accidentally had an orgasm while watching footage of a dictator being hanged. I hadn't meant to watch it; I'd simply flipped on the news. Oceans away, he swung something through me. To each his own special goneness, I suppose.

I received a message from your father today, telling me, perhaps you are already aware, that they plan on sending you on. Life support isn't the bargain it used to be, apparently. After I heard the message, I fell fast asleep. Then I woke suddenly again, and thought with a strange, panicky hope: *I'm going to be happy amid all this soul-robbery, you fuckers. One bright morning, I'll stand above the herd and make my voice heard.* Then I wrote a spiritual I will never sing:

> I'm thankful you gave mankind its brains,
> Its ability to breed.
> I'm accepting my words are all for naught,
> For I know you cannot read.
> (trumpet solo)

It was then I wished you could carry my body back to the West, where you are. I'd be alive. I'd keep myself alive—I promise—I just want to be carried, that's all.

Here are some final recommendations: Always keep to the middle of the road, always stop for the freights, always keep a sharp lookout, always keep a blade in your pants, always wear shoes you can run away in, always write your will before traveling, always thank the buzzards as they carry you off, always leave a little for the next day, always say goodbye with your face already on the other side.

I've been getting steadily drunker, and I'm now going to tell you a story: Once, a man and a woman had a conversation on a stone bridge. The river beneath the bridge was green, polluted, and toxic, but the water had some place to go; it ran swiftly through the city on its way to somewhere else. As for the two people, the lady was sickly and pale, and the man was not so sickly or so pale, but one could not say, upon seeing him on the street, "That man is healthy." Although they had not met before this afternoon, both had ruined their health looking for things that they were unable to find. The woman, whose speech was often interrupted by a raking cough, had lost her child, a boy, who had fallen off this same bridge when he was young, which was many years before. The man, his loss less severe, had dropped his gold ring into the river as he adjusted his tie, crossing the same bridge several weeks before. "What will you do when you find your child?" said the man. "I'll teach him not to disappear," said the woman. "What will you do if he leaves again?" said the man. "I'll teach myself to disappear," said the woman. "What will you do when you find your ring?" "I'll return to my life," said the man. "I'll reunite with everyone I've pushed aside." "What will you do if it leaves you again?" said the woman. "I'll drag them all along with me," said the man. Both unsatisfied with their answers, the man and woman tried to impress one another with miraculous visions. "Look," said the woman, "I see seventeen angels skimming over the water." "Look," said the man, "I see a bicycle cycling with no rider upon it." "Look," said the woman, turning bashfully to the man, "I see a child sleeping in the river with a ring around his finger." "My ring is not in the river," said the man angrily. "Neither is my child," said the woman angrily. So the woman went her way, and the man went his way, and only once did they look back to see how the other was getting along. The water beneath the bridge did not show any sign of having known it was the cause of their sorrow; it kept flowing. The man and woman are still alive even today: mad, wretched, and searching.

This is not the usual way in which this story is told. It is usually presented as a riddle: *A child sleeps soundly with a ring around his finger. He knows every secret, every one. And if he is not in the river, where, then, is he hiding?*

If We Should Ever Meet

PLEASE READ: I want to tell you before you begin that there are moments in here when I talk more about my family than the strange thing that happened to me, and if you're in a hurry, you can skip over them without losing very much of the story. I don't want to waste your time, and it's too late for me to change anything. Thank you.

I came in on a bus from the north. In my previous town, I worked in a building that was so tall that people used to jump from the roof when they became so sad that they wanted to end it all. One day I was sitting at my desk next to a window when I felt this shadow fall across my face. It was only there for a second, and I really didn't think much of it, but then someone I worked with came into my office and told me that somebody had just jumped off my side of the building, and asked if I saw it. I told him I had, even though I had only felt the shadow, and I became so guilt-ridden about saying this that I took a long time off work, just lying around in bed trying to figure out if that dead person was angry with me for making a memory out of him that wasn't true. When I finally decided that the person was probably furious with me, that I would have to live my life with the lie just eating at my heart as a punishment, my work called to tell me I was fired. So, getting off the bus in my new town, I made a vow to myself that I would try to view each new situation as independent from all the previous ones, and make no snap judgments, because although I had visited once before, I was unfamiliar with the people and customs. When my brother got home from the war, before they sent him out again and he got killed, at dinnertime my father and mother and my brother would all gather around the table, and before we started eating, my brother, who was a lot older than me, would lead us in a song he wrote called "If We Should Ever Meet," which became a little controversial within the family because the lyrics were vague and kind of ominous, and nobody could ever understand why he was singing about a meeting with strangers when there we were, all of us around the table, a family and not strangers at all. This is what I brought with me in my suitcase when I came to town: a toothbrush and a comb, a notebook and a pen, a dressy shirt for a job interview, casual clothes for hanging around, and all the money I had left, which was around five hundred dollars in cash that I kept in my shoe to confuse anyone that tried to rob me. In my previous city I had often worried about being robbed with a gun in my face, and my plan, should this have happened, was to tell the robber that I had a good bit of money, then take off my shoe and dump the cash onto the ground. While the robber was confused and stooping to pick up my money and poking around in my shoe for more, I would very quietly run away and avoid a gruesome fate. The first couple weeks in my new town I stayed in a motel under the freeway across from a veterans hospital, which wasn't so glamorous, I admit, but they offered affordable weekly rates for travelers on a budget. In fact, the only ugly thing I found in the motel was a big bloodstain under the bed, which I noticed while looking for a cracker that I had dropped, but before I let this discovery affect me, I decided that if I'd just been a little more careful in lifting the cracker to my mouth, I never would have found the stain. True, it would have lain there, bloody and silent, beneath me as I slept, but who is to say it wouldn't have worked on me anyway? Even so, I remembered my vow, and left it at that. The motel made a good effort at being a hot destination. Out front, it had a pool in the shape of a heart which overlooked the expressway, and I would have liked to dip a toe in had it not been November. The Jacuzzi was initially inviting, but I never got a chance to use it because it had been cordoned off by police tape ever since I had arrived. I managed to live pretty frugally: cheese and crackers for breakfast and dinner, and oranges for the Vitamin C. Finding a job was the only thing I thought about; I studied the classifieds like they were sacred scriptures, and even did fake interviews with myself in front of the mirror for practice. In the mornings I would shower and shave with a disposable razor and soap, which was sometimes tricky because I tend to grow hair inconsistently, at inordinate speeds along different parts of my face. The motel had complimentary toilet paper, so I was able to staunch any of my cuts with little folded scraps before I left my room. One day though, I was in such a hurry that I cut myself under my nose, bad enough that I had to ask the manager nicely for a Band-Aid. People gave me nasty looks on the bus that morning, and I only figured out why, when, after I had filled out an application at a coffee shop and was using the bathroom in the back, I noticed that I had a pretty sizable amount of blood in my teeth, which I wasn't able to taste because of the cinnamon gum I was chewing. My brother's song went something like: *If we should ever meet, I will kindly take your hand. If we should ever meet, I will cudgel every lamb. If we should ever meet, I will wear my cleanest gown. If we should ever meet, I will set fire to this town. If we should ever meet, I will deny those close to me. If we should ever meet, I will feign to disagree.* My first couple of weeks in town, I applied to about eighty percent of the town's businesses. I submitted applications at restaurants, toy stores, electronic stores, video stores, supermarkets, office buildings, bars, shoe and watch repair shops, cell phone stores, music stores, banks, home furnishings stores, department stores, and money lending stores. During this time, when I was still really new to the town, no matter where I was at noon, I would try and find a family restaurant to have some lunch. I would sit at a table for an hour, studying a map of the town, highlighting any streets I had not yet seen. I'd eat as much as I could. Most places didn't allow you to take food out, so I chose things from the buffet table that would stay in my stomach the longest. Cheese sticks, or a rare chicken fried steak seemed to work the best. My brother used to tell me that eating was one of the saddest things to take pleasure in because it is impossible to keep filling yourself once your stomach is full. I never saw many actual families in the restaurants, but there was never any shortage of seniors. Most of them didn't speak to one another; they just ate and puffed on their cigarettes and sometimes coughed for long stretches. Before I began any meal at those restaurants I would say a prayer in which I thanked God that I was still youthful, and still had some traces of ambition and the pleasant good looks my parents gave me. My mother didn't often speak to me when I was young, but one day I remember her giving me a pretty mild smile and telling me that some people were naturally transient, and she was pretty sure I would be one of them. She said she was basing her assumption on the fact that my father gave me half his blood, and he couldn't stand to stay in the same room for longer than a few minutes. My father used to come home once or twice a year, usually out of money and needing a shave pretty bad. He used to draw me up in his lap, even when I was a teenager, and whisper stories about boxcars and what he called ladies of the night. In town, the places I applied at were always willing to give me an application, even if there were no actual customers milling about. I had a fancy pen that I kept from my old job, and I used it to carefully fill out my applications. I would always, always write my name but leave the address box blank, because I didn't really feel comfortable telling anyone that I was living in the motel. I did, however, list the hotel's phone number, and next to it, in parentheses, I wrote to ask for me. I always made up my references, because although I'm sure some of my previous employers in my previous cities and towns would have gladly recommended me, I never did keep track of their phone numbers, so I figured it was better to list an imaginary person with a plausible number than a real person with no number at all. The owner of a laundromat told me that I seemed like a smart person, but he said that not only were they not hiring, he had reason to believe that there might not be any available jobs in the town, due to the economy and because everyone was living longer these days. I did wonder why he didn't tell me that until after I had taken the time to fill out my application, but I did appreciate his honesty. My mother worked all her life in a bank and she died in her bed. My father lived on the road and died on a railroad trestle. That's what the letter said, so who knows. The only thing left to do, after I applied to all those places, was to relax in my motel and wait for the calls to come in. I took a lot of showers at night, which was pretty good for my complexion as long as I didn't make the water too hot. There was a soda machine just outside my door, and it took a lot of willpower not to spend my money on a Coke or something refreshing. The tap water wasn't bad, though it was cloudy and smelled a little like sulfur. I didn't watch much television, because when I do I forget time exists at all, and I've never liked the feeling, once I turn it off, that not only has time passed, but that it has done so without me being really present for it. One day, during my job search, I found this little paperback braced under a dumpster where a wheel was missing. The book was a remainder, so it had no cover or back—even the title page was missing. The book was a collection of stories about dogs, which was, I thought, a pretty original idea for a book. My favorite story was about a dog who was beloved by many people until it got some sort of illness and died. The story didn't bother to explain the disease, or the grisly details of its death, but it did go on to talk at length about how the dog managed, during its short time on earth, to have a positive effect on many people in the community, so the line to view the little casket streamed all the way around the block. I stayed in the motel during business hours all that week, waiting for the calls for interviews. I sat on the edge of the bed with my posture as professional as I could manage, reading that paperback and listening for the phone, which I kept within arm's reach. I ate my cheese and crackers and my oranges in this position and even urinated in the ice bucket to be on the safe side. On Friday I called the manager to ask if he'd forgotten to give me any messages concerning possible interviews. He told me he hadn't, and that I was behind on rent by a week. I was pretty tired of sitting in the motel, and frustrated at not getting an interview, so I put on my dressy shirt and some newer jeans and started walking toward downtown. The motel was along an empty expressway, which was surrounded on both sides by chain-link fences and no sidewalk, so I did my best to kind of stroll quickly along the shoulder of the road. To make sure the passing cars would see me I waved both arms above my head like the insane and desperate do, and the vehicles gave me a wide berth. I reached downtown after about an hour, and walked into a pretty fancy bar that named their drinks after celebrities, which made them kind of fun to order. As I said, I was a little frustrated by the fact that I hadn't received any calls for interviews yet, so I had about eleven drinks myself, mixing and matching types of alcohol just for variety's sake. Then I got to feeling that someone was holding a blowtorch to my head, so I excused myself and went to the bathroom and ran my head under the faucet and dried off on the sanitary towel. Then I started introducing myself to strangers, asking my fellow patrons if they knew anyone who was hiring. I was being really friendly, buying them drinks when they asked me to, but the only lead I could come up with was at the dog pound, and the guy who told me was laughing pretty hard and putting his hand up a woman's shirt when he recommended it. Then I remembered that I had already applied there, and I thanked him anyway. Once on the road, my brother took me to a burlesque show and he cupped the dancer's breasts in his hands and pushed them up and down, like he was a scale. I don't remember him smiling. I walked back to my hotel on the same side of the expressway, putting my arms up high, but not in a needy way. A convertible pulled onto the shoulder, and a man in an Eskimo jacket asked if I wanted to make a hundred dollars. I told him to wait a second, and I took off my shoe, and I admit I wasn't too surprised when nothing, not even a few coins came jingling out. So I said that I did, and he told me to get in. We got going up to about ninety, which was definitely breaking the law, and I asked him if he wouldn't mind putting the top up, because I had only my dressy shirt, and he had his fur lining. He didn't do that, so I slunk down really low in my seat and tried to avoid the wind. I evidently fell asleep, because when I woke we were still screaming down the expressway, and the man had his finger pinching the sensitive part of my neck, directing my head toward his jeans, where he was kind of lazily wagging his penis at me. He dropped me off in a dark part of town and directed me toward the mission. I tried to explain about my motel under the freeway but he told me to get out of his car in a not-so-nice way. I was familiar with the dangers of shelters, having stayed in them in other towns, so I smartly tucked the hundred-dollar bill back in my shoe. The walk was cold, though, and I kept stepping on broken glass, which is pleasant-sounding at first but then kind of painful if your soles are bad. Nobody was in the streets, and as far as I could tell nobody was watching me from the burnt-out buildings. The mission was on a corner under another freeway, and I was surprised to find that it, like so many other places, was completely cordoned off by police tape. The front door was open, so I did a kind of limbo under the tape and walked inside. There was a young woman about my age behind the desk, who was crying, and behind her there were the bodies of about fifteen or so homeless people, all dead and very bloody and lying in pretty unnatural positions on the floor. She told me that the mission was closed, and that a group of seventeen or so people had come in earlier that night and killed every homeless person who happened to be staying in the mission, and later set fire to the unemployment office. My brother was shot by people in his own squadron, who thought he was the enemy. Apparently he died too quickly to have any last words. I asked her where the police were, and she said that the police only showed up in that town to put tape around crime scenes, because funding was low. She was pretty attractive even with the dead bodies behind her, so I asked her if she'd like to come back with me to my motel, where I only had an orange or two left, but said she was more than welcome to them. She said she would love an orange or two, and so we called a cab and rode in the back together until we got back to my motel under the freeway. The cabbie told me that the total fare for two passengers was one hundred dollars, and I got the bill from my shoe and kind of dejectedly handed it to him 1.) because it was the last of my money and 2.) because I didn't have enough for a tip. The woman wouldn't tell me her name, and she sat eating both my oranges in front of the television without taking their peels off. When I came back from brushing my teeth, she was gone, but luckily hadn't taken any of my things. I lay down and slept about thirty-seven hours until late Sunday evening, and then I went out and walked north to the convenience store, away from downtown, holding my arms in the air. The clerk was out front smoking, and I had just enough time to stuff a few candy bars in my jeans before he came inside. I browsed in the dirty magazines for a while, just to throw him off, and then I walked out. When I got to the expressway, I started to run. At the motel I found my suitcase sitting on the curb, all packed, and my room locked tight. I rang the night bell for the manager, but no one came to the window. I ate the remainder of the candy bars in frustration, and then laughed a little at how rash I was acting. When my brother and I drove across country trying to not to think about our dead parents or get in a car accident, I would sometimes break a long silence by asking him a question, usually about gas mileage or where we were going to stay that night. He would always get a little angry with me, tightening his knuckles around the steering wheel as he told me that words are infernal things that should never, under any circumstance he said, be used loosely. Then I would start to laugh, because my brother was always so serious and because I knew that laughter didn't constitute language, and then he would tell me to stop even that, because laughter is derisive and there is always a target of your laughter, even if it's only yourself, and that is terrible. I started walking toward downtown with my suitcase in my hand, and I felt so terrible that I didn't even bother to put up my free hand. After about an hour I came to a park, which was not locked, and although it was pretty cold, I thought it might be a decent place to spend the night. Before I could even select a bench a group of about seventeen men dressed in rags and some old tattered flags came out from behind the trees and surrounded me and told me they had a proposition for me. They said: "You see, one of our boys is losing his will and is growing demented in his old age. No one has suffered more than this man, and so we, being his friends, wish to help ease his pain. Several weeks ago, when you arrived in town, our boy saw you walking near the hospital with your arms up in hopefulness, and he smiled at you for a while, but in that smile lurked a terrible knowledge because he recognized your face from a picture your brother used to carry in his wallet when they were deployed together in the same squadron. This was before our boy shot him by accident, and although many years in the past, the memory is deforming him, and he'd now like nothing better than to have a duel with you. Don't ask us the reason, it's just what he wants." I did try and make a run for it at this point, but they circled in closer around me and kicked me with their boots. They told me that if I managed to get away, they would hunt me until the day I died, no matter the town I decided to settle in. "Just as we have made it impossible for you in this town in terms of employment," they said, "so it will be in any future town if you do not comply." Then they lifted the man from behind the bushes, who smiled at me, but not in a sweet way. The bandanna he wore was all sooty and crusted with old blood. He handed me a silver pistol and told me to stow it away in my pants and he showed me that he had already done the same. Then we squared away at thirty paces, and one of the seventeen shouted, "Draw." It seemed like he didn't even try to unholster his pistol before I got him in the shoulder and he kind of crumpled to the ground. I felt bad about this, so I ran over to where he was and tried to staunch his wound with a piece of my dress shirt that I'd torn off. The seventeen all gathered around me, whispering to one another. Then they closed in and wrapped their fingers around my hand that held the pistol and helped me level it at his head. I pulled the trigger and it was done. They all thanked me individually, each shaking my hand and bowing, and told me I was in no danger and free to leave. Once their man stopped twitching on the ground, they pulled him away, his heels dragging along the concrete. I looked around for some warm things to cover myself, and found a couple newspapers and some cardboard. I lay down in the middle of the park, feeling not so good. I awoke as the sun rose, my feet numb from where the cardboard hadn't been long enough to cover, and I stretched and did a little jog around the park to warm up. I saw a man walking a tiny dog, and I approached them and acted like I was going to pet the dog, but instead I picked it up and draped it across my shoulders like a mink and I sang my brother's song to him in the voice of my brother, and then I lied and told him that the song was mine. He took off one of his walking shoes and shook out several hundred dollars, and I went directly to the bus station and took the first bus here, to this town. I have a lot of applications out, and the people at the mission are pretty good about delivering messages, so who knows. The public library has been kind about letting me use their computers. I have a long list of e-mail addresses that I've found just poking around on the web, which I'm going to send my story to, and tell them to pass it along to whoever might be interested. My father, when he was home and I was sitting on his knee in the kitchen, once asked me to fill him in on an adventure I had had while he was away. I started to tell him about something important from my life but he stopped me in the middle of the story and told me that I was a bad teller, and that I should probably just go ahead and join the military so I could be useful, which I didn't want to do because I didn't want to die. He said I hobbled around in the silly parts and didn't get around to telling the real stuff, which he thought was in the violence. His death was not peaceful, so I do hope it was at least interesting for him. One last thing: if we should ever meet, maybe you might take me in for a short while, help me get established in your town. I promise to be a gentleman and not try anything funny. I can keep myself entertained—you won't even know I'm there.

Whoring

Once, on payday, a young man named Pate and a young man named Larsen sat on the edge of Pate's unmade bed, eating dinner in Pate's apartment. Neither of the men were handsome, though Larsen was the cleaner of the two.

"This food is pitiful and nasty," said Pate.

"I like spending time with you, Pate," said Larsen. He stopped eating and put his food box down on the bed.

Pate lifted his food box and tilted the rest of its contents into his mouth. "Sometimes you make me feel like a rose bouquet," he said. "But that being said, I will never fuck you."

"I know," said Larsen.

"The very thought sends me wriggling."

"You don't have to explain."

"If you woke up tomorrow with the body of a woman, but somehow kept your winning personality during the transformation, we might be able to work something out. But as it stands now, no way no how."

"We don't need to sleep together to have a good time."

"Good," said Pate. "So what the fuck are we going to do tonight?"

Larsen stood up from the bed and sat down on the floor, next to Pate's legs. "Well," he said, "There's the bar. We could start there, have a few drinks, figure out where to go next."

"But we were there last night, and the night before. The whole place is one big shit smear, if you ask me. It's payday, for God sakes. I want to whoop it up."

"We could go see a movie. There are a couple playing right now that I would consider seeing."

"Movies put a hole in your head. Jerk your emotions around."

"We could go have coffee at a coffee shop," said Larsen.

"If we go to the coffee shop," said Pate, "we might as well go to the god-damned bar. At least at the bar we can whoop it up and nobody will look askance."

"Or, we could stay right here and talk," said Larsen.

"Talk about what?" said Pate.

"We could reminisce," said Larsen.

"Fuck that," said Pate. "Let's focus on the present."

"What do you want to do, then?"

"I say we go a-whoring," said Pate.

"Couldn't we just go to the bar? You could find a girl to hook up with there."

"There's a god-damned difference," said Pate, "between hooking up and a-whoring. You don't go to the bar with the intention of hooking up. You go with the intention to get yourself drunk and be among the community. The hooking-up occurs on account of lonesomeness. Now, when you go a-whoring, you go to the whorehouse with the express intention of sleeping with whores. If you get a little tipsy while you're there, well, that's just a little sideline bonus. No way you've forgotten the feeling of walking into a whorehouse, seeing them whores all in a row: like eating cake, for breakfast."

"It sure has been a long time since we went a-whoring."

"Haven't been a-whoring since Sonny got himself a girlfriend," said Pate. "Those were the good old days. Me, you, and Sonny, a-whoring till dawn."

"I miss Sonny," Larsen said. "The old Sonny, I mean."

Sonny had met Bessy at the bar and had fallen in love. He refused to see either Pate or Larsen now apart from her. At the bar, he and Bessy sat in a booth. They drank the same drink out of the same glass with two straws.

Pate rose from the bed and took off all of his work clothes, then walked naked into his closet. Several minutes later he walked out in casual clothes. "I'll bet we can rouse Sonny," he said. "Sonny has whores in his future."

Pate drove them in his car to Bessy's house. She lived several miles outside of town in a cabin paid for by her brother, who was very rich. Pate and Larsen got out of the car and walked to the cabin. They stopped under the window, where the blinds were raised a crack. They could see part of the bed and part of the floor, and a leg that dangled off the bed but did not touch the floor.

"Makes me sick," said Pate. "Probably spooning."

"Whose leg is that?" said Larsen.

"Fuck does it matter?" said Pate. "Either it's a leg belonging to a man that's about to go a-whoring or it isn't."

"How do we get him out here?" said Larsen.

Pate thought for a moment. "We talk to Bessy first."

"Why?"

"We convince her that Sonny needs to go a-whoring to get it out of his system, then she goes inside and prods Sonny for us. We talk to Sonny first and he'll refuse outright, on principle. Then we'll have a real scene on our hands. Now what would make a lady come outside before a man?"

"A baby crying?" said Larsen.

"That's it," said Pate. "Make that baby cry noise you do so well."

Larsen began to whimper, then lifted his voice into pealing cries. They watched the leg right itself on the floor. Then another leg came down to meet it, and the legs walked themselves to the door.

"Keep it up," said Pate.

They heard the screen door open and close, and Bessy appeared before them under the window. She wore a thong and carried a bottle of milk. She was beautiful.

"You always greet crying babies with thongs?" said Pate.

"Hi, Pate," said Bessy. "Hi, Larsen. I heard a baby crying out here, where is he or she?"

"Just us babies," said Pate. He and Larsen laughed. Larsen made the crying noise again.

"I've heard Larsen's impression before," said Bessy. "This was different." She poked around in the weeds and in the ditch, looking for the baby.

"We wanted to ask if Sonny could come out with us tonight?" said Larsen.

"Sonny's no prisoner," said Bessy. "Where are you going?"

"A-whoring," said Pate. "I believe in honesty first."

"You boys use protection when you go a-whoring?" said Bessy.

"Of course," said Larsen.

"Always," said Pate.

"Well," said Bessy. "Seeing as a-whoring is just about the only thing Sonny and I can't do together, it'll make it all that more special for him."

"Can you go inside and prod him?" said Pate.

"Sonny doesn't like it when we prod him," said Larsen.

"I'll prod him and send him along," said Bessy. "You boys have fun tonight."

Pate and Larsen said goodbye to Bessy and walked to the car. Pate told Larsen to sit in the backseat. They sat in the car together with the heater on, waiting for Sonny.

"Bessy is really considerate," said Larsen.

"Immodest, though," said Pate. He honked the horn.

After a while, Sonny appeared in the headlights. He wore a fur coat, and was slightly better-looking than his friends. He sat down in the passenger seat.

"Howdy, stranger," said Pate. He started to drive to the whorehouse.

"Hello, Sonny," said Larsen.

"Bessy tells me we're going a-whoring," said Sonny.

"Sure are," said Pate. "You know what day it is, don't you?"

"Bessy has me all turned around," said Sonny.

"It's Friday, for your information," said Pate. "Friday and payday. What kind of shit coat is that?"

"It was a gift from Bessy," said Sonny. "I like it."

"I guess it's good to have you back," said Pate.

"It's good to be back," said Sonny, yawning.

"Are you too tired to go a-whoring?" said Larsen.

"Oh, no," said Sonny. "I'm just waking up from nap. How are the both of you?"

"Same old," said Pate.

"You been going a-whoring without me lately?"

"No," said Pate. "Hasn't been the same."

"How's your life, Sonny?" said Larsen.

"All in all," said Sonny, "pretty terrific. Bessy and I are very happy. We're even thinking about getting married."

"You do that," said Pate, "and you say goodbye to a-whoring forever."

"I don't know," said Sonny. "Bessy is very open-minded."

"Once that ring's slipped on," said Pate "the gloves come flying off. Ask Larsen."

"There's a good chance she'll restrict you," said Larsen.

"What makes you and Larsen authorities on women's ways?" said Sonny.

"Because me and Larsen are smart," said Pate. "What the hell do you think they pay us at work for, anyway? They don't pay us to stay ignorant, that's for sure."

"Well," said Sonny, "if you really think Bessy will lock the gate on me, I won't wear protection tonight."

"Not even the thin ones?" said Pate.

"Just me and the whores," said Sonny, "close as can be. It'll be a proper farewell."

"Aren't you getting your share of intimacy with Bessy?" said Larsen.

"Certainly," said Sonny. "We're as intimate as a whisper. But we certainly aren't close."

"Bessie wants you to wear protection," said Larsen.

"I'll wear protection for her any time after tonight," said Sonny. "But tonight I'm putting me first."

They arrived at the whorehouse. It was twenty stories high, with a whore's face in every window. They parked in a space near the dumpster.

"Why do you they need such a large dumpster?" said Larsen.

"The spent protection," said Pate.

"It feels good knowing I won't be contributing to more trash," Sonny said. "With the environment like it is."

"Any way you might reconsider about the protection?" said Larsen.

"No," said Sonny. "No, there isn't."

"Let's whoop it up, then," said Pate.

The men agreed to meet each other a few hours later on the front steps. Then they went inside and whored for a while. Later, Pate and Larsen met on the steps outside the whorehouse. They were tipsy and tired.

"Where's Sonny?" said Pate.

"Still a-whoring, apparently," said Larsen.

"Having a hard time letting go," said Pate.

They gave Sonny another hour. Larsen began to nod off on the steps.

"Did you see him in there while you were a-whoring?" said Larsen.

"Once," said Pate. "He was on all fours, whooping it up."

"Was he using protection?"

"Couldn't tell from my vantage point."

"We promised Bessy he would," said Larsen.

"We told Bessy that *we* always use protection," said Pate, "We didn't make any damn promises about Sonny."

"You're right," said Larsen. "But I do think we owe it to her to tell her that Sonny won't be home for a while. I'm exhausted."

"Me too," said Pate. "Fully unloaded."

They drove to Bessy's cabin. She was sitting in her thong on the porch, combing her beautiful hair.

"Hello, boys," she said. "Where's Sonny?"

"Sonny's still a-whoring," said Pate. "We're tired and want to get some damn sleep."

"You boys use protection tonight?" said Bessy.

"Sure did," said Pate. "Why do you care?"

"I'm not an idiot, boys," said Bessy. "I know where whore babies come from."

"You're talking over our damn heads," said Pate.

"I know that when a man and a whore are intimate, without protection," Bessy said, "that a whore baby is made. What the world does not need is more whore babies."

"Hadn't considered that," said Pate.

"Do you remember, earlier tonight, when I was sure I heard a baby crying out here?"

"That was just Larsen," said Pate. Larsen made the noise again.

"Actually," said Bessy, "you're wrong. After you took Sonny away, I heard the crying again, so I walked in the direction of it. Sure enough, there was a whore baby splashing around in the creek, crying his head off. It was the fourth one this week."

"Who did it belong to?" said Larsen.

"Nobody," said Bessy. "It was a whore baby. I gave it some milk and sent it on its way."

"I've never seen a whore baby," said Pate.

"Nor I," said Larsen.

"Of course you haven't," said Bessy, "They're invisible to men who go a-whoring. May I borrow your car, Pate?"

"What for?"

"I'm going to fetch Sonny."

"Best of luck," said Pate. "A man a-whoring is a man hell-bent." He handed Bessy his keys. "Can Larsen and me catch forty winks in your cabin?"

"No," said Bessy. "I don't trust either of you enough."

"We won't search for incriminating things," said Pate. "We're too damn tired for that."

"My cabin is messy," said Bessy.

"I don't feel well at all," said Larsen. "I really need to lie down."

"Alright," said Bessy. "But no fucking."

"Never was a possibility," said Pate. "Was just telling Larsen tonight, no way no how."

"Poor Larsen," said Bessy. "Larsen never gets what he wants."

"You're doing a good thing," said Larsen, "trying to keep more whore babies from being born."

"I know," said Bessy. "It's a thankless job." She let them in the cabin and drove away in Pate's car.

The cabin was furnished with two chairs and a bed. The only place to sit down was the bed. Bottles of milk took up every other inch of the place.

"I need to lie down," said Larsen. He flopped down on the bed. Pate sat at the edge, next to Larsen's legs.

"You think she's telling us the truth about the whore babies?" said Pate.

"I don't know," said Larsen.

"Makes me thankful I always use protection," said Pate. "Hate to think I was a Daddy without knowing it, to an orphan whore baby no less."

"I'm feverish," said Larsen. "Help me get out of these clothes."

Pate took off Larsen's clothes for him, and stared at Larsen's body. It was covered in lumps.

"Motherfucker," said Pate. "You got the lumps."

Larsen looked at his body. "I can't believe it," he said.

"You sure you wore protection?"

"I doubled up," Larsen said.

"They say it isn't foolproof," said Pate. "Boy, are we never gonna fuck now. Sorry, Larsen."

"I think I'm dying," said Larsen.

Pate took off his own clothes and checked himself for lumps. "I'm clean," he said. "Thank you, Jesus."

"I'm glad it was me instead of you," said Larsen.

"You think the lumps are doing you in?"

"No," said Larsen. "It's just general deterioration. I've known about it for a long time. I just didn't want to worry you."

"What a relief," said Pate. "I'd hate to give up a-whoring on account of some killer lumps going around."

"You'll be fine," said Larsen.

"Can I get you anything?" said Pate.

"I'd like some milk, actually."

"Sure thing," said Pate. He lifted one of the bottles to Larsen's lips.

"Lie down next to me," said Larsen.

"I'll sit with you," said Pate.

Pate took off his clothes and sat down next to Larsen. He was careful not to touch him, letting both his legs dangle off the bed. Pate fell asleep. Hours later, he awoke to a crying noise coming from outside. Then he heard laughter, and Bessy and Sonny walked into the cabin. They were drunk, knocking over milk bottles before they found the light and turned it on. Sonny was dressed in a tux-edo. Bessy wore a white gown.

"Hello, Pate," said Bessy.

"Hello, Pate," said Sonny.

"Hey," said Pate. "You hear that crying outside?"

"No," said Bessy. "There was no crying. Sonny and I were looking at your legs through the window, laughing."

"Why were you laughing?" said Pate.

"We expected you to be fucking," said Bessy, "and when we saw your two legs on the floor, we knew it wasn't happening. We were laughing at Larsen's misfortune."

Pate pointed to Larsen. "Little fella didn't make it."

"What got him?" said Sonny.

"Basic deterioration," said Pate. "The lumps are unrelated."

Bessy noticed the empty bottle on the bed. "That milk was for the whore babies," she said.

"Was Larsen's dying wish," said Pate. "Couldn't really refuse him."

"Fine," said Bessy. "We have plenty."

"You get married?" said Pate.

"It's official," said Sonny.

"The same night you fathered whore babies?" said Pate. "You make me ill."

"I wore protection after all," said Sonny. "It just didn't feel right without it."

"Sonny and I have been talking," said Bessy.

"And?" said Pate.

"Would you like to get intimate with us?" said Bessy.

"One last romp before the honeymoon?" said Sonny. "Might be interesting."

"Fuck no," said Pate. "I'm going a-whoring."

He took his keys from Bessy's hand and walked out to his car. He drove to the whorehouse, walked inside, and was never heard from again. After they buried Larsen, Sonny and Bessy went on to have and raise normal babies. They lived happily in the cabin until the end of their lives.

And I don't mind telling you another story, but first you'll have to pay for more time.

Five Didactic Tales

1. THE LONESOME VEHICLE

Not long ago, a young man with a keen sense of injustice lived in a house all by himself in the country. The place in which he lived, however, was not so remote that he couldn't see his neighbors' houses when he stood on his balcony and drank his tea. Below the young man's balcony sat a little driveway in which he parked his car. His car was very old, and would sputter and cough each time he turned the key. One winter's day, the young man's car finally failed to start, and he bitterly said goodbye to it and had it towed away to the junkyard, where he knew it would rot and become estranged from him.

The next morning, while drinking his tea, the young man noticed a very lonesome vehicle parked in the same place, where his old car used to rest. The vehicle and all its many windows were painted entirely black. From his balcony the young man looked left and right and then straight ahead, and thought that perhaps the lonesome vehicle belonged to one of his neighbors. So after much pondering the young man walked to the west and knocked upon his neighbor's door, where an old woman greeted him.

"You are the young man who idly stands upon his balcony," she said.

"Yes," said the young man. "Do you own the ominous vehicle which rests in my driveway, where my old car used to sleep?"

"What color is the vehicle?" said the old woman.

"It is black as the asphalt in Colorado," said the young man. "Does this ring a bell?"

"I have been twenty years blind," said the old woman. "I only asked so you might paint a pretty picture for me."

So the young man walked to the north and knocked upon his neighbor's door, where an old man greeted him.

"You are the young man with more time than the Lord," he said.

"Yes," said the young man. "Do you own the lugubrious vehicle which rests in my driveway, where my old car used to sleep?"

"What are the dimensions of the vehicle?" said the old man.

"Wide as a dinghy, long as a shark," said the young man.

"I'm afraid you shall have to try again," said the old man.

"Spatiality eludes me," said the young man. "It looks like any other vehicle, save for its blackness and inherent sadness."

"Well, I drive a high, threatening vehicle," said the old man. "But her color is blue."

So the young man walked to the east and knocked upon his neighbor's door, where a little child greeted him. "You are the young man whom I have worshiped from afar," it said.

"Yes," said the young man. "Do you or your guardians own the vexing vehicle which rests in my driveway, where my old car used to sleep?"

"Fool," said the child. "Can't you see that myself and my guardians haven't the money for vehicles?"

"But you live in such luxury," said the young man. "Your house looms large."

"There is *nothing* beyond this exterior," said the child, rapping upon the doorframe.

The young man returned home and inspected the lonesome vehicle, all the black windows, all the wiring beneath. He pulled on the four doors, but the four doors were all locked. In frustration he called the authorities and read them the license plate.

"The vehicle belongs to somebody," replied the authorities, "but unfortunately we collect information rather than dispense."

In frustration the young man called the towing company, who sent someone out to tow the lonesome vehicle.

"I can't haul this vehicle," said the towing man, "for it was I who towed the vehicle here from the forest, on the orders of a little man who said he lodged with you. It is highly likely that you stood upon your balcony contemplatively drinking tea while all of this was going on."

After the young man had sent the towing man away, he began to violently search the entirety of his house. He knocked over tables, scattered sofa cushions, and put his fists through lampshades. Then he looked beneath his bed, where there lay a little man with fearful eyes.

"Ah," said the young man, "you must be the owner of the loathsome vehicle which rests in my driveway, where my old car used to sleep."

"I am," said the little man.

"Why are you under my bed?" said the young man.

"Ostracized from my dwelling in the forest," said the little man, "I sought refuge in a country home. I noticed you on your balcony one day, unhurriedly drinking tea, and thought I might incur very little of your wrath should you discover me. So I stayed here under the bed until night, when I nibbled at little leftover morsels, and even took a bath while you slept. I also conducted myself quite nobly when you brought a woman home from the tavern and you said immaculately vile things to her while in bed."

"The only thing that concerns me," said the young man, "is that an upstanding little man such as yourself should be ostracized from his community. You may lodge with me as long as you wish, but tomorrow we will drive to the forest and together we will raze your little community until nothing is left, because if there is one thing I cannot tolerate, it is injustice."

"Agreed," said the little man, and they both slept, the young man on his bed, and the little man beneath.

That night snow began to fall, and in the morning a heavy layer blanketed the ground. After tea and a light breakfast, the young man and his little friend entered the lonesome vehicle, and although the little man's legs hardly reached the pedals, they were soon on their way. But on the interstate, they soon hit a stretch of black ice and found themselves in a ghastly accident. There was no hope for the young man: he died at the scene.

News of the accident spread quickly, and soon all the young man's neighbors arrived, followed by the authorities and the towing man. The little man gave his statement to the authorities and watched as the towing man towed his vehicle to the junkyard. He was then placed in chains and returned to the forest, where his community, having heard news of his deed, welcomed him as a hero.

2. THE GREAT HOUSE

Once, in the east, a newly married couple shared a great house on a large plot of cleared land, which was bordered by a dark forest. The couple had no children, and would often promise one another, after exercising or lovemaking, that there would never be any children.

The forest beyond the house was populated by the destitute and abject, and so to keep them from the great house the married couple employed several of the destitute to build a fence that protected the property and hired several of the abject to stand watch, equipping them with large firearms.

Often, on summer nights, when the couple would entertain, their guests would become frightened by the drumming and chanting emanating from deep within the forest, and so, as the nights passed, the guests, one by one, failed to accept their invitations, until the day when the couple was left, save for the guards, to themselves.

One night over dinner, the husband, who had swallowed several glasses of wine, suggested to his wife that they might have some children to brighten the empty rooms of the great house.

"When the forest has overtaken our great house," said the wife, "then we will have our children."

The couple soon retired to bed for lovemaking, but the husband in his disappointment and the wife in her portentousness could only manage an awkward embrace, and soon they fell fast asleep.

The next morning the husband wandered down to the property's edge and approached a guard who stood shouldering his rifle toward the woods.

"Let me ask you," said the husband, "how much has the forest moved today?"

"Not a grain of an inch," replied the guard.

"Very well," said the husband. "Have there been any sightings today of the dwellers?"

"Not a coattail of a garment," replied the guard.

The husband kept this information to himself that night at the dinner table. “How was your day?” he asked the wife.

“My day passed as any other,” she said.

“In time we might change that,” he said, lovingly patting her hand.

The next morning the husband returned to the same guard, whom he now favored for his honesty. “How much has the forest moved today?” he said.

“Not a hair’s width from yesterday,” replied the guard.

“Will the forest ever consume my great house?” the husband said.

“Perhaps in the time of your grandchildren’s grandchildren’s grandchildren,” replied the guard.

“Very well,” said the husband, who was about to return home, but hesitated as a faint noise caught his ear. “The drums,” he said. ‘The drums and the loud lamentations. Do they seem closer to you?”

“I hear no drums nor loud lamentations,” replied the guard.

“Very well,” said the husband, and he returned home.

That evening, the husband and wife sat down to dinner. “How was your day?” said the husband.

“My day passed as any other,” said the wife, “except that I suddenly was able to perceive the distant drums from within the confines of our great house.”

“I thought so,” said the husband. “I thought I heard them too.”

The next morning the husband again spoke to the guard, who appeared slightly nervous at his post.

“The noises are becoming louder,” said the husband. “How do you explain this?”

“There must be a celebration within the forest,” said the guard.

“But the sound is so mournful,” replied the husband.

“They are very sad people,” replied the guard.

“Is that not them dancing just behind the first row of trees?” said the husband.

"My eyesight is leaving me," replied the guard. "You might need to hire another."

"Very well," said the husband, and he returned home.

That evening the husband and wife sat down to dinner. "I learned the origin of the noises today," said the husband.

"Yes?" she replied.

"The people of the forest are having a party," said the husband.

"You know it makes me sad to hear that word," said the wife, bittersweetly patting his hand.

That night the couple said a prayer in which they thanked a higher power that they had each other and a great house to live in.

The next morning, there was an uprising in the forest, and by noontime the destitute and abject had armed themselves with stones, ropes, and firearms, and soon had taken the fence, slaughtered the guards, and overrun the great house. Easily captured, the husband and wife were paraded about the compound in chains, and fed rainwater and grubs of the forest for their meals. By nightfall they were tried for malfeasance and found guilty and sentenced to hang at midnight, side by side, from a beam above the wide porch.

As the nooses tightened around their necks, the husband said: "The forest has overrun our great house. Certainly now we might have our children."

The wife looked out over the crowd of hateful faces. "Yes," she said. "I don't know."

3. THE FAST MEAL

During a time of great wealth in the country, a number of those who had plenty took to the forest, where they lived in self-inflicted poverty in the hopes that they might get back to the marrow of experience, which had long since vacated human life.

One day, a widower, who lived in the city with his three middle-aged sons, decided such a change might be beneficial, so he sold the house and all of their belongings, liquidated his mutual funds, gave his monies to several pet charities, and, in order to symbolically finalize this severing, pushed the family vehicle over a nearby cliff.

When he had finished, he wiped his hands on his slacks and said to his sons, "I fondly remember in hallucinatory fragments the essence of human life, which you were born too late to know. We will go to it now, and feed upon it."

The sons, who had grown quite comfortable in middle age, became very moody, and voiced their misgivings. Although none worked, all had busy schedules, and so they said to their father, "You elders with your mad and flickering visions. You will drive this generation to ruin! It is only you who fear time's passage, only you who inhibit our fun. Why not let us live the life promised to us as wealthy citizens of this country?"

"The forest still holds revelatory potential, no matter how debased our dealings with it have heretofore been," said the father. "Furthermore, what kind of father would I be if I denied my sons the access to the wisdom of the ages? I would be the kind of man that the Good Lord, His infinite mercy notwithstanding, would not, and should not, let die."

"Very well," said the eldest and youngest sons, who were sympathetic, in a sniveling way. "We do not hear what you say, but we hear the way in which you say it, and we wish to remain in your good graces, because we love you."

"Brothers, you appall me," said the middle son. "If you follow our father to the forest, you will never again be able to order a fast meal. Therefore, I will stay behind, with some close friends, and curse the three of you while I enjoy fast meal after fast meal."

"Then you shall be dead to us from this moment on," said the father. "We will think of you as we think of all the dead that infuse our every moment: bitterly."

"Yes," said the two other brothers. "While we do recognize the virtue of your argument, we have never really liked you, and will therefore say goodbye."

So the widower and his two sons began walking until they came upon a store teeming with outdoor goods. Inside, they piled their shopping carts with breathable clothing, backpacks, bug repellent, soft fleece jackets, sleeping bags, rods with which to fish, and a variety of dehydrated foods. The father happily walked along the aisles with his sons, sipping a cola he intended to pay for upon leaving. At the checkout counter, the sons assumed looks of wishfulness, smiling at their father in the hope of financial assistance. Their father examined his pocket, but then remembered that in his haste to prepare for the essence of human life, he had thrown his billfold into a garbage can.

"You," said the father, pointing to his younger son. "Though perhaps not without ambition, you have proven in your years to possess the weakest manual dexterity, which might disincline you to forest living, so you shall stay behind and work menially for this establishment until the sum is paid off. Keep your backpack handy and I will, if necessary, send for you." With that, the father signed an IOU, packed the equipment, and set off for the forest with his eldest son.

After several days of walking, the father and his eldest son became submerged in foliage, and were it not for the passing voices of similar travelers, both would have thought they had left the world completely behind. Their days were spent walking with their heavy loads and their nights were spent cooking their meals slowly over a little stove. One night, the father noticed that, as he watched the lentils simmer, his eldest son carried a very gloomy expression on his face.

"Son," said the father, "give me a digestible version of your troubles."

"I miss so many things," said the son. "I miss the city and the pretty girls, our home and our car and the smell of gasoline."

"I might remind you that this here is the essence of human life," said the father, tasting a lentil.

"However," said the son, "I could forever go without these things and only cling to their memories . . . if only I could eat a fast meal again. It's insufferable, waiting for these things to cook."

"Just one fast meal?" said the father.

"One more," said the son, "and I will be quiet and perennially grateful."

"And if I should refuse for the sake of purity?"

"I will abandon you and rejoin society. As much as the idea of you wandering alone creates a dull and nameless ache in my chest."

"You have convinced me," said the father. "Tomorrow we will cross a paved road, if my memory is honest with me, and if we follow that paved road but a mile, we will come to a place that sells an acceptable fast meal, and you shall eat one."

The eldest son became quickly happy, but his expression soon fell. "But father," he said. "We haven't a penny for a fast meal."

"I am currently forming a plan," said the father. "In the morning I will strip from my outdoor clothes, and I will cover myself in brambles and leaves and smear my face with earth and at the place that sells the fast meal I will pretend to be impoverished and insane. There being still an abundance of sympathy among men, they will not deny me a meal."

The next morning they reached the crossroads, and there the father stripped off his outdoor clothes and pressed his face into the mud and rolled about in the leaves and brambles. He went on down the road, affecting a limp, while the son waited with both of their packs. "How quickly I'll savor my fast meal," the son said to himself.

Very shortly after, the father returned with a paper bag leaking grease and a cold cola in a paper cup.

"And you have eaten none of it?" said the son, beside himself with joy. However, even through the caking of mud on his father's face, the son could detect a reddening in the cheeks.

"It's true I have a certain predilection for cola," said the father. "In my excitement I may have imbibed three sips."

The son embraced his father and ate his fast meal so quickly that his father did not even have an opportunity to ask for a bite. Satiated, the father and his son began walking back into the foliage.

Soon, however, the son began to feel ill, for his fast meal contained sour meat, which bored holes in his insides, so he began digging a hole in the forest floor with a small spade. He continued digging until he had before him a hole six foot by three, and then the eldest son lay down in the hole and quietly died.

Mournfully throwing earth upon his son, the father said a short prayer, which the Good Lord did not hear, for He was sleeping. An angel was keeping watch, however, and noted the sudden suffering of the old man in a ledger, which was full of the names of individuals in the world undergoing similar bereavement.

The father, leaving the shallow grave, dressed in his outdoor clothes, washed his face in a little stream, and returned carrying both backpacks to the outdoor store, where his youngest son had been promoted to middle management, and was not so pleased to see his father.

"Your backpack is packed," said the father. "Your brother has perished. Won't you leave everything you love and give me the pleasure of your company as we discover the essence of human life?"

"You say my brother has perished," said the youngest son. "Why should I follow you into the forest?"

"You have no health insurance," said the father. "You have no pension plan. I have reason to believe that you will climb no higher than middle management. They will fatten you with flattery and employee discounts, and when you become too old to lift the goods to the shelves they will slaughter you with a pink slip."

"You humiliate me on such a grand scale," said the son, "that I cannot help but be convinced by your insight."

So after several days of walking, the father and his youngest son were submerged in foliage, and were it not for the passing voices of similar travelers, both would have thought they had left the city completely behind. Their days were spent walking with their heavy packs and their nights were spent cooking their meals over the little stove. One night, the father noticed that his eldest son carried a very rancorous expression on his face as he watched the chickpeas boil.

"Son," said the father. "Tickle my old ears with gently phrased complaints. I emphasize *gently*."

"How did my brother perish?" said the youngest son.

"He was served ill meat by a local establishment that serves fast meals," said the father. "About a mile from here."

"Oh, what I wouldn't give for a fast meal right now," said the son. "Never in your ears would I ever again complain, if my belly could be full with a properly prepared fast meal."

"Your brother felt the same," said the father. "And that earned him death."

"Certainly I won't be eating the same meat," said the son. "I will gladly take that chance."

"And you promise to stifle any future whinings before they dribble from your lips?"

"I will be the son you desired when you saw fit to impregnate our dear mother the third time."

So the father told his youngest son about the crossroads and his disguise, and the son was filled with happiness. The next morning, they arrived at the paved road and the father once again stripped himself of his outdoor clothes and rolled about in brambles and smeared his face all over with mud. "I will order you a different meal than your brother," the father said, walking down the road with the affected limp.

"How appreciatively I'll eat my fast meal," said the youngest son to himself. Very soon after, the father returned with a large paper bag that was all spotted with grease and two plastic cups full of cola. A delicious smell wafted toward the youngest son, who was seated on both backpacks.

"I was unable to discuss your brother's fate with the management," said the father, "because my disguise might have been easily detected. However, so pathetic did I appear to them this time, the tears I have cried for your brother having surely mined new wrinkles in my face, the clerk showed extraordinary pity, sending me off with not only your meal, but a small side of beans and a drink for myself."

Both ate their meals at the crossroads, and before they were even thirty paces back in the foliage, the son began to feel ill, for his fast meal contained old meat, which thundered through his insides, and he set to digging a hole in the forest floor with a small spade. He continued digging until he had before him a hole six by three, and then the youngest son lay down in the hole and quietly died.

Dejectedly throwing dirt upon his youngest son, the father said a lengthier prayer, which the Good Lord did not hear, for He was pondering larger matters. The same angel was keeping watch, however, and with his pen poised above his ledger, ready to record the sufferings of the father, he suddenly decided to alert the Good Lord of the father's uncommon level of suffering. He queried the Good Lord for his advice, but it was clear by His deep, musical sighs that He did not wish to be bothered.

The father, leaving the shallow grave, changed into his outdoor clothes once again and washed his face in a little stream. Then he began to wander the forest, but before long the air grew cold and the night fell quickly over the land. After many hours of walking, the father, caught in an abrupt downpour, came to a clearing where there dwelled many people of means from the city. They reclined in padded folding chairs under a blue tarp encircled around a roaring fire. Over the rain and wind the father could faintly hear a man and woman trading verses from a song:

> How nice to be so warm and snug
> With children and a wife.
> Come join our circle as we enjoy
> The essence of human life.

The father, hearing their words, rushed into the tent and began doing violence to anything near his feet. He was quickly subdued by broad-shouldered men and women and children, whose muscles had grown taut from forest living. They stripped the father of his outdoor clothes, emptied and feasted upon the contents of his backpack, dragged him through the mud, tossed him in thorny brambles, and then sent him on his way.

He walked all night until he reached the crossroads, and he then took the paved road out to the establishment that served fast meals. "I will order the fast meal and join my sons," the father said stoically to himself. In his misery he forgot to drag one of his legs behind him as he walked.

At the counter, the father had scarcely caught his breath, when the clerk spoke.

"I know you from not long ago," said the clerk.

"You absolutely could not, for I am destitute and insane," said the father. "I have no home but the hearts of my fellow man, and have walked impossible distances. I have no money, yet I hunger for a fast meal."

"I have no fast meal warming under my lamps for you," the clerk said.

"Bad meat," the father said. "Bad meat will suffice."

"Neither good meat nor bad of mine shall you ever eat," said the clerk, "for this establishment has a strict policy that does not condone charity beyond two occasions. Yours, sir, are used up."

The father then wandered alone in the forest for many years, cold and impoverished, eating what he could of the berries that grew from the bushes and drinking turbid water from the little streams. On the day he was certain he would die, he spoke aloud a rambling and rather unrehearsed prayer, which the Good Lord did not hear, for He was busy feasting. The same angel, although he'd recently discarded his ledger because it had grown so overstuffed and inky, heard the prayer, and taking pity on the father in his frozen wanderings, he went straightaway to a local weaver, giving her specific instructions for the garment he had in mind. At twilight that very evening, the angel flew down to the father and wrapped him in the blanket the weaver had woven, which was embroidered in gold stitching with the words "the essence of human life."

"Get thee to the city," said the angel to the father. "Stand outside the outdoor store, and proclaim what you have seen."

The father, however, was beyond admonishment, only gazing silently at the angel with unfocused and dimming eyes.

"Very well," said the angel, who then stretched his glowing arms around the father, and lifting gently, carried him up into the night sky and beyond, into the crowded and somewhat dank bosom of the Good Lord, where the father was greeted coolly by his wife and two sons.

Expertly prepared fast meals were the featured item that night at the Great Feast, and the father consumed one after another, until he forgot that he had ever hungered at all, and then the angel took him gently by the arm and led him to his appointed room.

4. THE VENGEFUL MEN

Not long ago in another country, a civil war raged between the governing party, who believed mankind descended from the stars, and the multitudinous poor, who believed mankind descended from oxen. One day a man and his wife, both of whom were poor, received news that their only son had been captured and subsequently beheaded after a skirmish in the south. After many nights of uninterrupted grief, the woman suddenly roused her husband and said to him, "Where might we go to avoid death ourselves, to live quietly and somewhat ambitiously?"

"Though being a vengeful man," said the husband, "we will leave this loss behind us and move to *another* country, where we will open a little store."

"What will we sell?" the wife said.

"We will stock our shelves with chintzy goods and sweet-tasting snacks," said the husband.

Within a week they had sold their home and all of their possessions, save for their clothes and a few toiletries, and arrived *here*. If they had not arrived *here*, this story would have no reason for being told, for what is significant only happens within the confines of our great borders.

So after several weeks of language training, the husband and wife soon opened a little store in the downtown area of a little city. The day they opened their doors to the public, their shelves were fully stocked with plenty of chintzy goods and sweet-tasting snacks. The little store did quite well, for there was plenty of foot-traffic downtown, and no citizen of a great civilization can resist spending his pocket money on throwaway things, as long as they be properly advertised.

One very cold afternoon, during a particularly busy shift, the light from without suddenly shifted, the aisles of goods became darkened, and the wife noticed through the window an old desiccated man sitting in a wheelchair in front of the little store. The sun hovered almost directly behind him and threw a looming shadow over the little store and all its shoppers, who quickly filed out.

For many days this was repeated, in the afternoon when the sun was low, and the little store suffered greatly in profit. When both the husband and wife realized the great harm the crippled old man was causing them, the wife opened the door and spoke to him. "Who are you?" she said.

"I am a fifth-generation resident of this town," said the old man, "but injured in a war, without home or friend. I carry with me at all times the missed connections section of the local newspaper, and suspicious beliefs concerning outsiders. I warn you, I am a highly bigoted and vengeful man."

"The shadow you cast is scaring away our customers," said the wife. "Will you hurriedly come inside where it's warm? Or never pass this way again?"

"I might," said the man. "Though I won't pretend to enjoy myself."

"My husband and I had a son who was killed in a war. He was younger than you, and it wasn't your war."

"I will come inside," the man said dejectedly.

Soon enough, the old desiccated man had made himself quite comfortable next to the register, and the shadow being gone, the customers began filing back into the little store. With a twinkle in his eye, the cripple regaled the passing shoppers with stories from his history, and when in the presence of the husband, told little offensive jokes about foreigners. The customers, secretly hateful of their reliance on foreigners for disposable trifles, laughed and laughed.

"Who is this decrepit old man sitting beside you, who so deftly conjures up our basest feelings?" they asked.

"I do not know him," replied the husband angrily. "He carries with him a terrible shadow."

That evening, as the husband and wife began to close the shop, the husband approached the old man. "The hour is come for you to leave," he said. "Go away and do not pass this way again."

"I will spend the night and all future nights in your little store," said the old cripple. "You may plug me in to one of your outlets, and I will snack from your well-stocked shelves. If you turn me out now, I will surely die in the cold, and will make a point of doing so in front of your little store, for I am a highly vengeful man. Your customers will see me slumped there in my chair, overturned in the gutter and frozen to the bone, and they will suspect foul play or at the very least a niggardliness of charity, and they will condemn your little store and you and your wife will go bankrupt and be forced to wander."

So the old desiccated man got his way, and the husband and wife plugged his chair into their outlet and locked him in the little store. Later that evening over dinner, the wife detected her husband's misgivings about the old man. "It is a difficult situation, I know," she said. "But we are unfamiliar with the codes and customs of this country, and it might be best to wait and see."

"We have seen our homeland torn apart by sectarian violence," the husband said. "The graves of our ancestors looted as if they were no more than the aisles of a lowly store. The body of our only son, I needn't remind you, has been buried apart from his head. So now we are *here*, and an old abject man wishes to deprive us of our profits. If we let this pass, we are a shame to our people."

"What would you see done?" said the wife, who placed a hand over his.

"Tonight I will surprise him in the little store and cut off his head," said the husband, and abruptly left the table. The husband then procured himself a blade from the garage, and kissed his wife goodbye and left for the store. All night the wife tossed and turned in her bed, for her husband had not returned. When the violet rays of dawn came falling on her window, she heard the front door open, accompanied by the noise of stamping footsteps and a high-pitched, mechanical buzzing. The wife entered the kitchen, where there kneeled her husband with the old crippled desiccated man seated in his chair. Both regarded her seriously.

"We have come to a remarkable understanding," said the husband, passing his wife the blade, "that this problem is more ours than yours." The old cripple began nodding solemnly, and then both men suddenly bowed their heads. "We only ask that you make it quick," they said.

5. THE STRANGE NURSE

A nurse was serving on the western front of a popular war. She went out one morning into a smoking field, strewn with the dead and dying of both sides, to administer aid to those who were in need.

First, a male soldier, whose blood was seeping from the places where his eyes had once been, called to her.

"Medicine," he said. "I need medicine."

"I have no medicine," said the nurse. "How about a vision?"

"A vision will do."

She sat down in the mud beside him and cradled his head in her arms. "Somewhere, not far away, a stadium stands atop a high hill, lit up and waiting for something coming."

"Thank you," he said, and died.

The nurse walked on until a female soldier, blood seeping slowly from both ears, tugged at the hem of her long skirt.

"Water," the soldier said. "I need water."

"I have no water," the nurse said. "How about a song?"

"A song will do."

She knelt and began to sing:

Take my hand, I'll lead you away
Outside the fracas, above the melee
Where the fruit is ripe and the water is clean
Won't that do wonders for your self-esteem?

"Thank you," the soldier said, and died.

The nurse walked farther across the smoking field until a little drummer boy, blood seeping from the stumps left where his hands had been blown away, waved to her.

"Medal," he said. "I need a medal."

"I have no medals," said the nurse. "Shall I make you one?"

"Making one will do," he said.

The nurse went searching across the wide field until she found one of the drummer boy's hands. She brought it back to him, and kneeling, pinned it to his shirt. "Handsome and manly," she said.

"Thank you," said the drummer boy, and died.

The nurse suddenly became tired, and wished to be back home. And so she persisted and walked a little farther until she reached a grove of blackened trees. There she was approached by a pack of wolves, who walked on their hind legs and lolled their tongues at her.

"What are your intentions?" said the nurse.

"Oh, we wish you would turn back," they said.

"And why is that?" she said.

"We'll miss watching you work," they said.

"But I must return home," she said. "I am needed there."

"And where is that?" they asked.

The nurse winked, and then revealed that she wasn't a nurse at all, but one of God's angels in disguise.

"Forgive us," said the wolves, disbanding and leaving her alone.

Moral: You never know.

Repenting

Braines lay in prison, repenting. When he was finished, he thought of his friend Handy, who was in the adjacent cell. Handy was a co-conspirator, and Braines' best friend. He crawled to the hole he had dug to Handy's cell, and peered in. His eyes met Handy's through the hole.

"Thought you might be up," said Braines.

"Knew you were up," said Handy. "Didn't hear you kicking."

"Quit it," said Braines. "Didn't hear you chewing."

"Kicked it," said Handy.

"Prison's got a way of flaying away the habits," said Braines.

"Sure does," said Handy. "I'm a shell of my self. Been a while since we spoke."

"Sure," said Braines. "I ain't been inclined."

"Me neither," said Handy.

"How about Churn?" said Braines. "Any contact?"

Churn was the other co-conspirator, and Braines' other best friend.

"Churn ain't been inclined neither," said Handy.

"And how do you know that?" said Braines.

"Ain't seen him," said Handy.

"What you been up to?" said Braines.

"Little of this, little of that," said Handy.

"Slim few things a man can be up to in the wee hours," said Braines, "especially in the wee hours."

"I've been repenting," said Handy. "Don't you go judging me."

"Hush now," said Braines. "Nothing wrong with repenting. Was doing a little of it myself tonight."

"It don't feel too good to repent," said Handy. "Us being killers and all."

"All part of the plan," said Braines.

"Say what?" said Handy.

"Repenting's like falling down a well," said Braines. "Whole time you're repenting, you're falling, but there's a bottom to the well, you bet. You know what happens when you hit the bottom?"

"No," said Handy.

"You're dashed against the damn stones, and you're nothing but a shell, but you gather your strength, and by and by you get fired up to commit more crimes."

"How far have you fallen?" said Handy.

"Must say the bottom is pretty nice," said Braines, "if a little dank." He laughed his old laugh. "You catching what I'm wafting?"

"Caught it," said Handy. He laughed a similar laugh.

"How far down are you?" said Braines.

"Pretty close," said Handy. "Could use a little extra gravity."

"Go repent a little more," said Braines. "I'll wait here."

Handy slid away from the hole. He crossed his legs, closed his eyes, and started to murmur. Then he opened them again. "What's the plan?" he said.

"That it?" said Braines.

"That's it," said Handy. "I told you I was close."

"Good man," said Braines. "You fired up?"

"Melting," said Handy.

"What about Churn?" said Braines. "Churn up?"

"Let me check," said Handy. Handy crawled to the hole in the opposite wall, and then crawled back.

"He's reading," said Handy, "Ain't no telling how far he's fallen."

"What's he reading?" said Braines. "Ain't but one book I know of here."

"Couldn't tell," said Handy. "He looked engrossed."

"Better not be the Good Book," said Braines. "If he's reading that, he's got a ways to go."

"You never know with Churn," said Handy.

"True," said Braines, "Muteness is mysterious."

"What do you want to do?" said Handy.

"Well," said Braines. "I was thinking the world might've forgotten about us. That it might be time again to remind them who we are."

"Don't know about the forgetting," said Handy. "Our crime was downright heinous."

"If you couldn't remember your damn alibi on the stand," said Braines, "how do you expect to know whether the world can or can't remember what we did?"

"You didn't remember your alibi too well either, as I remember," said Handy.

"I played my part," said Braines. "I was supposed to be the dumb one, remember?"

"Churn didn't fare so well either," said Handy.

"You'd think that a mute wouldn't give nothing away," said Braines. "But Churn was as obvious as a hospital visit."

"That's all in the past, Braines," said Handy.

"You're right," said Braines. "Besides, Churn's indispensable to the group."

"What are you thinking?" said Handy.

"One thing's for sure," said Braines. "If I repent any more, I'm gonna immolate before I even make it back to the world."

"Me too," said Handy. "So?"

"Give Churn the sign," said Braines. "I'll call the guard."

"Guard's not going to be happy about us leaving," said Handy. "Gonna miss kicking us around."

"Never laid a hand on me," said Braines. "I painted pictures for him in my spare time."

"What kind?" said Handy.

"Renditions of the crime scene," said Braines. "Extra ghastly."

"Glad you were treated fairly," said Handy. "That's rare."

"Don't you worry about me," said Braines. "Me and the guard are on good terms." He laughed his old laugh again.

"Where should we meet?" said Handy.

"You really have to ask me that?" said Braines. "Where's the only place left where a man can be free? In this region, at least?"

"Don't know," said Handy.

"The woods, Handy," said Braines. "The woods are still wild."

"Free seems to me the best way to be," said Handy. "See you in the woods."

"Repent some more in the mean time," said Braines. "I need you good and ready."

"Best of luck," said Handy. "If we don't meet, you'll know they got us."

"Worse ways to go," said Braines. "You'll make it. You and Churn."

"Churn's unsteady sometimes," said Handy.

"Churn'll find his legs," said Braines. "I'm tired of jawing."

"Alright," said Handy. "See you in the woods."

Handy's eyes left the hole. Braines lay back and thought about what he would miss. Nothing, he decided, and he started repenting, though it was just for show. After a while, he called the guard, who came to the door.

"Yes, Braines?" said the guard.

"Time to make good on our special relationship," said Braines.

"I'll miss you," said the guard.

"You'll miss my ghastly paintings, is what you'll miss," said Braines.

"I will," said the guard. "But mostly I'll miss jawing with you."

"Open up, now," said Braines.

His cell door swung open, and he walked into the empty hallway. Handy and Churn's doors were also ajar. He saw all the other prisoners in their cells, either lying back or repenting. Braines laughed his old laugh as he passed out of the prison and jogged the hundred miles to the woods.

He found his co-conspirators in a clearing, on a picnic bench. Handy was watching for passersby. Churn was reading by starlight.

"How's the weather on the coast?" said Braines.

"Coast is sunny and clear," said Handy.

Braines approached them and gave Handy a quiet high five. "Any problems?" he said.

"Had to drag old Churn out of his cell. Wouldn't leave without his book."

Braines inspected the book. "Damn it all," he said. "It's the Good Book."

"You remember reading that when you were littler?"

"Fairy tales," said Braines. "Childhood sugar dreams."

"We could try and wean him off it," said Handy.

"Wean him with what?" said Braines. "You got another book in your possession?"

"Something will turn up," said Handy.

Braines put his hands on Churn's shoulders. "Churn," he said. "This isn't gonna work. Got to put down the book. Got to put the book down or Braines and Handy aren't going to be best friends with you any more."

Churn put the book down. He looked bereft.

"He always listened to you before me," said Handy.

"Hell," said Braines. "Look at him."

"Brutal sight," said Handy.

"I can't look at him," said Braines. "When I do I see the person that I am and never wanted to be. Now Churn, if we let you keep reading your book, do you promise to do the dirty work for us, just like old times?"

Churn blinked.

"We got a deal," said Braines. "Get that book out of the dirt."

Churn picked up the book and dusted it off. He opened it and smiled.

"Braines," said Handy, "if Churn is still reading the Good Book, how can we be sure he's hit the bottom?"

"Unsolvable problem," said Braines.

"So what's the plan?" said Handy.

"Something'll turn up tomorrow," said Braines. "These are happening woods. We're bound to find some victims."

"You want to ditch the prison jumpsuits?" said Handy.

"God no," said Braines. "Less you're comfortable going à la carte."

"But what about the element of surprise?" said Handy. "The victims won't even give us the time of day if they see that we're repented and escaped prisoners."

"Good point," said Braines. "Can't have victims without the time of day. Let's turn 'em inside out."

They turned their uniforms inside out. Handy held the Good Book while Churn turned his.

"I'm hungry," said Handy.

"I'm downright feeble," said Braines.

They heard something cry in the trees. Churn picked up a stick and threw it in the direction of the crying. The crying stopped. He put down the Good Book and walked into the trees. He came back with food in his arms and dropped it on the picnic table. Then he picked up the Good Book again.

"There's old Churn," said Braines. He bent down and took a bite.

"Maybe Churn never had to hit the bottom," said Handy. He bent down and took a bite.

"What the hell are you talking about?" said Braines.

"Maybe Churn never felt the need to repent," said Handy, "because he doesn't even know he committed a heinous crime."

"I've had about enough of your epiphanies," said Braines. "There's food on the table. Ain't that enough?"

"I guess," said Handy. "Churn, bend down and get some of this."

Churn kept reading.

"He's a natural man," said Braines. "No doubt about it."

Braines and Handy ate until they were picking bones.

"I'm swole up," said Braines. He lay down in the dirt, closing his eyes. "Bedtime."

"Come to bed, Churn," said Handy.

Handy and Churn lay down in the dirt, next to Braines.

"All together again," said Handy. "Feels nice."

Braines fell fast asleep, and started kicking Handy and Churn. Handy slipped off to sleep, then started to chew. Churn lay on his back, reading the Good Book by moonlight.

They awoke in the daylight. Two men stood over them. "Get up," said one of them.

Braines shielded his eyes from the sun. "Get up Handy," he said. "Get Churn up too, while you're at it."

Handy got up. So did Churn, but he started reading.

"Morning, men," said Handy.

"Good afternoon is more like it," said the other man.

"We overslept," said Handy. "Damn."

"My name is Tone," said the first man. "Sorry to have woken you so suddenly."

"My name's Mace," said the other. "I don't know the word sorry."

Braines rubbed his eyes and looked behind the two men. He saw a third person near the trees, but couldn't tell if it was a man or not. It had very long hair and wore a dress. A straw hat hid its face. "Who's your partner?" he said.

"Please don't you worry about him," said Tone.

"So it's a him?" said Braines. He rubbed his eyes again. "You sure about that?"

"Don't think you're in position to know," said Mace.

"What's his name," said Braines. "Surely he's got one."

"He hasn't told us," said Tone. "If he tells you, let us know."

"Sure is nice to meet you both," said Braines.

"I'm Handy," said Handy. He stuck out his hand. No one shook it.

"Did you say your name was Handy?" said Mace.

Braines shot Handy a look. "No," said Handy. "I said my name was Randy."

"I could have sworn you said Handy," said Tone.

"Randy's the name," said Handy. "And these are my friends Bane and Chum."

Braines shot Handy another look. Churn kept reading.

"The radio's been talking a lot today about a Handy, Braines, and Churn," said Mace. "And, of course, it's also talking about the end of the world."

"Radio's always talking about the end of the world," said Braines. "Can't never stomach more than five minutes at a time, myself."

"Why are you worried about the end of the world?" said Mace.

"Don't like to think that we all gotta settle up eventually," said Braines.

"Why does that worry you?" said Tone.

"I'm having too nice a time amongst my friends, I guess," said Braines.

"Are you boys vacationing?" said Handy. "I hear these are happening woods."

"We are not," said Tone. "We met a few vacationers today, though." He and Mace laughed a hollow laugh. "What are *you* doing here?" said Mace.

"Vacationing," said Braines.

"Really?" said Tone. "Where are your tents?"

"We like to rough it," said Braines.

"Then where are your canned goods?" said Mace.

Braines pointed to the bones on the picnic table. "We like to rough it," he said.

"And the remains of your campfire?" said Tone.

"Chum here likes to read his book by the night sky," said Braines, "so we don't never light one."

"You believe our story?" said Handy.

Braines shot Handy a look.

"You believe the story we're telling you?" said Handy.

Braines shot Handy another look.

"You believe the justification for why we're here?" said Handy.

Braines shot Handy one more look.

"Hush now," said Mace. "We try and believe everything."

"We're very open people," said Tone.

"What do y'all do for a living?" said Handy.

"Move around," said Mace.

"We used to be the same way," said Handy.

Braines did not even bother shooting Handy a look.

"Well, what changed that?" said Tone.

"We had to get nine to fives," said Braines.

"Must be nice to take a vacation like this," said Mace.

"You bet," said Handy. "In such a camping spot to boot."

Braines looked again at the long-haired man in the hat and dress. He thought he recognized him. "Do you mind if I talk with your friend?" he said.

"Please give it a try," said Tone.

Braines walked to the third man, but the third man turned away. "Do you know me?" Braines said. The man did not answer. Braines walked back to the others. "Bashful, ain't he?"

"Sometimes," said Mace.

"He's tougher than he looks," said Tone.

"Not with that hat, he ain't," said Braines.

"You must think you're funny," said Tone.

"What?" said Braines.

"You and Sandy," said Mace. "You like to make jokes, don't you?"

"Never judged a man for laughing," said Braines.

"Your jokes must be very important to you," said Tone.

"Jokes are a perfect escape," said Mace.

"Never thought humor was my specialty," said Braines.

"It really isn't," said Mace. "So don't worry."

"He's right," said Tone. "Do you know why?"

"No," said Braines. "Not sure I care to."

"Because when you're funny, you can make up for deficiencies in your story," said Mace.

"We should be getting along, Bane," said Handy. "I don't like the way they're talking to us."

"We met a lot of people today," said Mace.

"Yeah," said Tone. "The vacationers all pretended to be criminals, and all the criminals pretended to be on vacation."

"Been nice meeting y'all," said Braines.

Mace turned toward the third man in the hat and dress, who was curling his hand toward the trees. "Handy," said Mace. "Our partner wants to introduce himself to you."

Handy looked at Braines, and Braines gave him the sign. Then Handy started jogging away from all of them, as fast as he could. Tone and Mace drew weapons, and shouted at Handy, who froze. "Alright," he said. He began walking toward the third man. Braines watched them walk together into the trees.

"Chum," said Braines. "I need you to put down the Good Book and look at these men."

Churn put down the book. He looked at the men. He smiled.

"What the shit, Chum?" said Braines.

"How are you, Churn?" said Tone.

Churn said nothing, because he was mute.

"Y'all know Churn?" said Braines.

"Churn here used to do our our dirty work," said Mace.

Churn smiled broader. Braines saw the long-haired man in the hat and dress come back to the clearing.

"Me and Churn and Handy all repented in prison," said Braines.

"So you *were* in prison?" said Tone.

"Now seems like a time for honesty," said Braines.

"Why?" said Mace.

"Don't know," said Braines. "Sometimes a man just knows."

"And you did a lot of repenting there?" said Mace.

"Sure did," said Braines. "Handy too. With Churn I can only guess."

"Repenting's a wonderful thing," said Tone. "Not many are willing to do it."

"It's such a nice gesture," said Mace. "But your crime wasn't really that bad."

"It was heinous," said Braines. "I'm just happy you fellas remember it."

"It must have been heart-wrenching," said Mace, "being falsely imprisoned like you were."

"We had a fair trial," said Braines. "We deserved every bit of that punishment."

"You can believe what you want," said Tone.

"If it makes you feel better," said Mace.

"I don't feel good at all," said Braines.

Braines saw the third man begin curling his hand toward the trees.

"He wants to get to know you," said Mace.

"Please don't keep him waiting," said Tone.

"Me and the Devil are on good terms," said Braines. "He'll recognize me."

"Good for you," said Mace. He and Tone put their weapons in Braines' face. "But our man's no devil," he said. "He's worse than that."

"Tell me one thing," said Braines. "Would I have been safer back in prison?"

"No," said Tone.

"We were headed there next," said Mace.

"What if I hadn't repented so much?" said Braines.

"Wouldn't have meant a thing," said Tone.

"So there was nothing I could have done differently?" said Braines.

"Nothing," said Tone.

"You did as well as anybody," said Mace.

"Will you take care of Churn for me?" said Braines.

"No," said Tone.

"Churn is next," said Mace.

"Let him come with me," said Braines. "Please. He's got no friends. All he's got is that damn book."

"Our partner takes one at a time," said Mace.

"Hell," said Braines. "Goodbye, then." He started walking toward the long-haired man in the hat and dress. Then he looked back and waved at all of them, though it was just for show. Tone and Mace didn't wave, and Churn had gone back to the book.

Braines took the third man's hand, and let himself be led out of the clearing, into the trees.

"Do you know me?" said Braines.

The third man lay Braines down in the piles of the others, then closed Braines' eyes for him. The question was never answered.

The New Year

Early one morning, a long time ago, I was bathing in the Okeh River, near downtown Hernville, gently scrubbing the most neglected parts of my body with an old bandana I had recently acquired. And though I was alone, and the water was cold, I kept myself warm by remembering all the memories I had made the night before, when I was out on the town, ringing in the New Year in style. And when I had finished replaying all those memories, and each, in their own way, had brought me a small flicker of warmth, I found that I still had more of myself to cleanse, so I changed the direction of my thinking, from memories to more tangible items, and began listing all the things I was thankful for in my life:

1. The recent return of my health.
2. The range of my mobility.
3. The fact that there was always someone listening to my prayers.
4. The fact that I had not been murdered at any time the past year.
5. My couch.

And once I had finished listing these things, I found that I still had a few more crevices that needed attention, so I continued scrubbing, working the bandana over myself as quickly but as industriously as I could, even as I felt my arms and legs losing feeling. And finally, realizing that I really was fighting a downhill battle, knowing that in order to save my precious life I would have to emerge from the water before I got myself to a level of cleanliness I could live with, I tried, in one last push, to distract myself again, and began formulating some resolutions for the New Year, hoping they might grant me that last bit of warmth I needed to finish, but before I could even begin to envision the year ahead, and all that I might accomplish in it, I heard a voice call down to me from way up on the bridge.

"Hey," it said. "I know what you're doing."

"I'm just taking my bath for the day," I said. "No big deal."

"Didn't look like bathing to me."

"Oh, don't pretend to know anything about my morning routine."

"Looked like frolicking," he said. "And my name is Moany."

"Well," I said, "if you were down here, you'd be able to see clearly," and while I wholeheartedly agreed with what I was saying, I instantly regretted saying it; I didn't really feel like engaging with Moany, or any one at all, for that matter, especially after having such a social time the night before.

"I still say you were frolicking," Moany insisted, as he—a little recklessly, I thought—stepped sideways down the steep embankment to meet me. Once he reached the riverbank, I looked at him closely to make sure he was safe to associate with. Much to my relief, Moany was thin and little. I would really like to pay him more tribute in my description of him, because of how nice a person he was, but he was quite ugly. His only possession, beyond his clothes, was a little jar full of clear liquid that he kept under his arm.

"What made you think I was frolicking?" I said.

"You were waving your hands around."

"I was cleansing myself," I said, suddenly feeling my muscles beginning to spasm. "It's too cold to be frolicking."

I then told him then that I would talk a lot more candidly if he would give me a moment to get out of the river and put on my outfit: my jeans and my jacket. Moany was silent, though he seemed to understand my needs, politely turning away as I emerged from the river. After I was dressed, I invited him to join me on my couch. When I'd first moved under the bridge, there was plenty of unoccupied space for the taking, but at the same time, there wasn't any real cozy spot I could call my own—a place where I could sleep, eat, and get some thinking done, while not constantly having to readjust my position due to the sharp stones on the riverbank. So I really was overjoyed, and at the same time, very humbled, when, one day, on the bridge above me, a head-on collision occurred between a furniture truck and a truck carrying combustibles, and as a result of the tragic accident, a smoky but brand new leather couch tumbled down the embankment, end over end, until it came to rest, right side up, at my feet.

"Say you were frolicking," said Moany. "What would you have been frolicking for?"

"I don't know," I said. "Maybe I would have been frolicking at the fact that we have a new year upon us."

"And why would that be cause for frolicking?" said Moany.

"I'm not sure," I said.

He offered me a drink from his jar, which was full of tepid tap or perhaps river water. I drank one sip, and then told him that I would be fine for a while. I was particular about my drinking water.

"I had a pretty good time last night," I said.

"I'm not sure I like sitting here," Moany said. "You better hurry up and tell me about your New Year's Eve."

He really wasn't the kindest of listeners, but it was rare that I had one at all, so I kept going. "I was downtown for the festivities," I said. "Usually, I stay here under the bridge during holidays, because they tend to get me a little down, and I don't like having to put on a public face when I'm having trouble wearing my private one. But last night, though I was feeling just about as down as ever, and though I tried to sleep it off, all the exploding fireworks kept snapping me awake, and I decided that if I was going to get through the night I needed to be around some kind—any kind—of life, so I went down to Big Square. I also decided that I wasn't going to let my mood spoil anyone else's that night: as I walked, I put on a smile, and held it there, and if ever I felt it slipping a little, I would do my best to raise it back up for the benefit of those around me. There were crowds of people there, in Big Square, all dressed in costumes and acting out of character in a fun way, and with my wide smile I think I fit right in. The strange thing was, at some point—right around the time a complete stranger gave me a paper bag with a party hat, a noise maker, and a warm bottle of beer inside—I realized that the public face I was wearing was equal to my private one, that the smile I was smiling was actually genuine, and that I was having a good time without even trying. And after that, I found that my legs were more limber than I was used to them being, and I started to dance, first just by myself, but then with everyone close by, until, gradually, a circle formed around me, and I saw that every public eye had fallen on me and every smile was directed toward me." Moany's face began to darken when I described the dancing—out of jealousy, I supposed. I started to think twice about continuing with my story. He was in pretty bad shape.

"Go on," he said. "It's fun for me to live through your fun."

As long as he was willing to hear it, I really was more than happy to tell it. "Well, by the end of the night, I was up on people's shoulders, and they were telling me that they were going to make me their king, and all sorts of other friendly promises that I never really expected that they would make good on. And then the hour grew really late, and I found that my only company left in Big Square was the garbage that people had left behind, and I came back to the bridge, still smiling wide even though I was alone."

Moany didn't make any real effort to hide his frown. "That does sound like a good time," he said. "Have you ever had a girlfriend?"

"I don't know," I said. "There was an old woman who used to lean over the bridge and show me her breast every day for a while, but I'm not sure if you would count that."

"I wouldn't count that," said Moany.

I sensed a sad story coming on and shifted my hips a little lower into the couch to get more comfortable.

"While you were out dancing with the crowds," Moany said, "my girlfriend and I were roaming the streets, doing our dancing act for money."

"I've always wanted to dance professionally," I said. That I haven't really is one of the major regrets of my life.

"It was just regular dancing," he said bitterly. "I would lie on the concrete, my girlfriend would press play on the boombox, then she would climb on my back and sway. When I couldn't take her weight anymore, I would tap her ankle and we would switch."

"Moany," I said, "I am not a dancing authority, but it seems like this dance was very simple."

"We tried the more elaborate stuff before," Moany said, "but no one donated. So we settled on the dance I just told you about. Ugliness is in, anyway. And we did well last night, until the boombox broke. After that, we started to head for home."

"Where do you live?" I said. I wanted to make sure he still knew that I was interested in him and his story.

"My girlfriend and I live in Balltank, not far from here. We live under a bridge, pretty much the same as this one. Last night, my girlfriend and I were walking home after making a good amount of money, and we passed by a shop, where we saw the most magnificent dog in the window. I asked my girlfriend several times how much she thought the dog cost, but she assumed I wanted to buy the dog, and told me that we needed a new boombox before we went ahead and got a pet. But that wasn't what I wanted at all. I just wanted to know the price of the damn dog, just to get an idea. She told me if I went into the shop, she was going to leave for the electronics store without me and start shopping for a new boombox. I didn't believe her, and went in the shop, and I found the manager in the back. He had more dogs around him, but none were as good as the one in the window. I asked him how much the dog was, and he kind of sniffed at me and told me I couldn't afford it. I told him I didn't want to buy it, but that I wanted to know the damn price. He told me fourteen dollars. I was satisfied, for the moment. When I left the store, the streets were empty, and I found my girlfriend at the electronics store a couple blocks away. She was talking to a clerk and choosing between two boomboxes. She asked me for my opinion, but I didn't want to give it. I was just thinking about the dog. I told her that even though the manager at the shop sniffed disdainfully at me at first, he quoted me a price of fourteen. She still thought I wanted the damn dog, even though I told her again that I didn't. Then she held up two boomboxes and told me to pick, and I told her I'd rather get the money we made that night and take it back to the shop and just show the manager that we could afford the damn dog. She told me that if I went back to the shop with the money that she would leave me and I could find my own way home. Like a fool, I ripped the money out of her hands and ran back to the shop, which the manager had closed, and was locking up. I showed him the money and proved that my girlfriend and I could afford it, but he told me to put my money away because he'd just sold the damn dog to a loving owner, and when I asked him if he could see that I could have afforded the damn dog in the window, he told me that he didn't give a damn. He made me really upset."

"Some people really don't want to get to Heaven," I said, though I felt bad about casting judgment on a person who was only real to me as a character in Moany's story.

"You're right about that," said Moany. "But it gets worse. When I got back to the electronics store, my girlfriend was gone, and so was the clerk, and by the time I made it back to the bridge in

Balltank, they were already done making love, and were talking sweet to one another. I knew I had no say, and the whole thing was my fault, so I gave the money to my girlfriend and started walking. I made the Hernville city limits just as the sun was peeking up, and then I saw you frolicking as I was crossing the bridge."

"What did the dog look like?" I said. "I was not frolicking."

"The dog in the window was beautiful and proud," he said. "I'd seen others that good in my life, but not for a long time."

"Moany," I said, "Tell me the truth. Did you really want to buy that dog in the window?"

"No."

"It's OK if you did. Sometimes I want things that I shouldn't have, like a big brass bed, for example, instead of this couch. I think that's pretty normal."

"I didn't," Moany said, "and what made me leave my girlfriend was I realized that no matter what, no matter how long we stayed together or how many people we entertained over the years, I knew I'd never be able to convince her that I didn't want that damn dog. Now, if someone would have given me the damn dog for free, I certainly would have cared for him, but I just couldn't justify spending money on him, beautiful as he was. "

"What do you do now?" I said.

"I don't know," said Moany. "I don't know, and I don't really care what happens."

"You're depressed, aren't you?"

"I guess so."

"The doctors at the clinic will give you free trial packs of medicines," I said.

"What clinic?"

"The one in Big Square."

"I like medicines," Moany said, "when I can get them."

"Now, they don't always tell you what the medicines do, so you have to be careful, but I'm sure they could give you a couple of trial packs to experiment with until you find the one you like."

"How many medicines are in a trial pack?"

"Two or three tops," I said. I was happy to have gotten him off the subject of the dog. "And when they run out you can go back to the clinic, and if they have any more trial packs, they'll give them to you, no problem."

"What if they don't have any more of the medicines that I like?"

"Well, doctors and drug companies are always working hard to develop new medicines, so they'll have something comparable, I bet."

"What do you take?" said Moany.

"Oh, I don't take anything at the moment. I pray."

"You sure know a lot about medicines."

"Well, when I get really down, financially speaking, and when my prayers take a little longer to get answered than I had originally expected, the clinic lets me take out their garbage and restock the paper towel dispenser for a little change. The doctors try to push those trial packs on me, but I always tell them that trial packs don't put hot meals in my stomach."

"So are you saying I should pray, or go to the clinic for medicines instead?"

He had me in a tough spot. I had been given a lot of medicines from doctors before, and they did work pretty well, until the clinic had to shut down for a while, and I had to learn to live without them. It was hard, but I made it through, thanks to prayer. When the clinic reopened I didn't need the medicines at all, just the money they would give me for my janitorial work.

"I guess either some praying, or some medicines, or a combination of both would be good for you," I said. I wish I could have been more helpful to him, but at the end of the day, people just have this sad private pain that is impossible for anyone else to access. That's exactly why I get so excited about Heaven and its promises.

"The more I think about it," said Moany, "the more I realize how much I wanted that damn dog in the window. I don't know why I couldn't be honest with myself."

I wanted to respond, but thought there was a good chance that my words would not have been kind ones, so I started looking at the river, just watching the trash swirl around. When I turned back to look at Moany again, I was surprised to see that he'd taken a knife out from his pants. I thought there was only about a fifty percent chance that he was going to use it to murder me, given how little I had, but I didn't want to offend him, so I got up from the couch and casually pretended that an insect had bitten me under my jeans. But then Moany just kind of dragged the knife across his own throat, until he bled so much that he lost his balance and fell off the couch and onto the rocky bank. It was all over quickly. I really hope that was the most nonsensational way to tell you about the death of Moany. It was a surprising moment for me, and I wanted to make you feel my surprise, but not to the point that you thought I enjoyed talking about it. It was a terrible thing to see.

I buried Moany and the knife behind some shrubs that were growing along the bank. I really didn't know what to think. I had just met this man about an hour before, and we had had a nice conversation, and now here I was throwing the last of the topsoil over his bald head because his bandanna had come off in the fall. I began a prayer over his grave, a long and sweet one, because I thought that Moany, especially because he was able to admit his desire for the dog, deserved to get to Heaven. About three quarters of the way through the prayer, though, I got this spooky feeling, and I decided to stop, because the last thing I wanted was for Moany to wake up one fine morning in a place that he never wanted to be at all. Some people are scared of Heaven, and you have to respect that.

I tried to go about my day as I normally would: I cooked a modest breakfast, replayed all the positive memories from my life, and continued to list everything I was thankful for. I considered another bath in the river, but didn't feel like disrobing again, and besides, the morning had only grown colder since Moany's demise, so I settled for just rinsing the blood off my hands. After I dried them on my bandana, I got back on the couch and tried to take my mind off the image of Moany's empty eyes just staring at the dirt over him. I knew his brain was not getting oxygen anymore, but for some reason, I really believed that his eyes could still see. Before falling asleep for an afternoon nap, I was finally able to formulate my New Years resolutions. They were:

1. Bathe more frequently.
2. Establish better relationships with people.
3. Spend less time on the couch.

I don't want you to think that Moany had a negative effect on my life. And I don't want you to think that it was significant that Moany's death happened on New Year's Day. Actually, looking at it one way, although the relationship hadn't been given time to develop, I had already made a good start on keeping my second resolution. Really, all I mean to say is that Moany's death was certainly sad, but I was sure it didn't have any symbolic meaning or anything terrible like that. To the living, death doesn't bring symbols when it comes, it just brings death. But I also don't want to suggest that his death was meaningless, as some might argue. It might have been meaningless, in the grand scheme of things, but even now I find it hard to refer to Moany's sudden death that way. I'll say it this way: the meaning of Moany's death has yet to become clear to me, but I know one day it will.

When I woke up from my nap, I heard a man calling to me from the bridge.

"I love you," he said.

"I love you, too," I said. During all my years I lived under the bridge, I found that it was never a bad idea to respond in this way.

"I am the mayor and I want to speak with you," he said.

It isn't everyday that you get to meet a mayor, so I climbed up the embankment and met him on the bridge. He wore a suit and tie, but covered his face with a bandana—on account of the dust, he said—and spoke to me from behind it. Next to him sat a magnificent dog, and I immediately thought of the dog in the window. It might have been how well-behaved this dog was, or it might have been the fact that Moany's death was still fresh in my mind. It would have been an incredible coincidence if the same dog that Moany had seen in the window was not only now owned by the city mayor, but was also standing before me, in all its glory, so soon after Moany's death.

After I introduced myself, I asked about the dog. "That is a beautiful dog," I said. "I wonder how long you've had him."

"Several years," the mayor said.

"Oh," I said. That just about settled it. It wasn't the same dog, unless the mayor was a liar, and I don't think that he was, given how upstanding he appeared. But even if the mayor were a liar, I realized that it still might not have been the same dog. You might call this some sort of epiphany on my part.

"Are you a citizen of this country?" asked the mayor.

I nodded yes.

"Are you a resident of this state?"

Again I nodded yes, but was less sure.

"And you live full-time in this county?"

I nodded again.

"Are you happy with the life you lead in this city?"

I shrugged. "I had fun downtown on New Year's Eve."

"Do you know I'm running for reelection in the spring?"

I nodded no.

"Do you know why I think you should vote for me?"

Again I nodded no.

"Prepare for my stump speech," he said.

"I have a couch down there," I said. "I don't own it, but I think of it as mine, and I would be a lot more comfortable listening to you if I could sit on it."

He agreed, and we walked down the embankment together. I held on to his arm out of politeness, because he was pretty old, and because, as I've said, the decline was surprisingly steep. When

I was good and settled on the couch, I told him I was ready. He gave me his stump speech. It was like a prayer, a prayer better than any one I could have dreamed up, even if I had been given all the time in the world. I pledged my vote to him then and there. As repayment for listening to his speech, the mayor agreed to help me unbury Moany, just to see if his dog had any reaction to his corpse. But after all our digging, we found Moany's grave empty, and I realized with joy that he'd been called home to Heaven. Then, wouldn't you know it, right there under the Okeh River Bridge, the mayor gave me a job in his reelection campaign, where I was paid to stand behind him at his rallies, smiling a wide, mostly genuine smile and representing a hopeful, new kind of voter. After he was reelected, I had his ear for the first part of his new term, and made sure that the New Year's celebration that year was even more elaborate than the one before it. I want to end this positively, on my uplifting time with the mayor, because I know that these kinds of moments are the only things people remember from the stories that they hear. I want to leave you feeling good. But however you feel, good or bad, for some reason, right now, I feel the need to tell you that, selfish as it might seem, the most important reason why I am telling this is because I want you to remember me.

The Buddy

After school, Robert and Scott would wait at the bus stop with a crowd of other kids.

Sometimes Robert made lists of things that he should never say to Scott. One item that appeared regularly was, "I love you."

Robert was not handsome, but Scott was.

The truck was equipped with a noisy exhaust and painted bright red. A loudspeaker jutted from just above the windshield.

"You're a comedian," Scott would say to Robert. "Come on, be funny."

Robert was out walking the dusty path that ran beside Amoring Lake. He carried a sharpened stick, spearing anything he found clinging to the fence line.

He would have given anything to drive such a loud and threatening machine.

Although he did pushups before bed each night, Robert's build remained small—with the exception of his chest, where his fatty little breasts swayed under his shirt as he walked.

Scott was skating around in the gas station parking lot, jumping steps and abandoned tires. A younger boy sat watching him on the curb, eating an ice cream cone.

"What's up, Robjob?" Scott said.

"Just gonna try and buy cigarettes."

Scott pointed to the boy at the curb, who had chocolate running down his pale arm. "This is Stewart, my little brother."

He spoke in a reedy, frog-mouthed way, telling Scott dirty things about girls that happened to walk by. "Go put this banana you know where," he would say, or "I gotta put this tongue somewhere soon or I'll choke on it."

Stewart giggled, and held out a dripping hand. "Puterthere," he said. He giggled again.

Robert spied a piece of animal feces in the weeds. He smeared his right hand in it and bent low to shake hands.

A throng of kids stood at the bus stop beneath a budding elm tree. Robert had an erection—born of nothing—that had been with him since fifth period.

Stewart threw the half-eaten cone away and looked uncertainly at his brother. Scott was doubled-over.

"Robjob is the nastiest!" Scott howled. "The nastiest! Come hang out for a while."

On the south side of the intersection, across from the lake, stood the Shell station, where the driver of the truck was rumored to work.

He stood and waited with his hands clasped inconspicuously across his crotch, occasionally smiling at Scott. Scott stood anxiously on his skateboard, snapping his bubblegum.

The three of them walked down Fairfield in the late afternoon sun. Stewart ran ahead chasing butterflies, his curls flopping.

"Puterthere," he said, making the frog voice. "Puterthere."

Scott's house was dusty and cluttered and smelled of overripe produce. There were two cramped bedrooms, and in one of them, Scott shared a bunk bed with Stewart.

They saw the truck down the way. It sat idling in an intersection, behind a bent stop sign. Suddenly the truck roared and peeled out, spraying dust and gravel up onto the hoods of other vehicles. The boys around Robert began to lose control. "Oh, shit," they cried. "Holy shit."

Scott picked up a crusty-looking book off the floor, entitled *The History of Philosophy*. He thumbed through it. "Lots of cool ideas in there," he said. Robert asked to borrow the book, but Scott squinched up his eyes and said, "Nah."

"Hey guys," said the voice from within the truck. Some of the boys nodded. Others, unable to hide their enthusiasm, jumped and waved. The tinted window slid down.

Scott showed Robert his father's collection of dirty videotapes. Then they went to the backyard and scooped dirt into an old pie tin. They tried to serve it to Stewart, telling him it was chocolate.

He was neither old nor particularly young, and he held a PA in his hand and spoke into it. "Hey," he said, the nasal voice full of static, his finger stabbing through the open window. Robert turned to find that the driver had targeted Scott.

"My brother doesn't know a damn thing," Scott said.

Then they placed Stewart in the middle of the trampoline, and bounced him until he lost his footing and rolled off onto the concrete.

"You hang around the Shell station sometimes?" said the voice. "With that kid brother?"

"Sure," Scott said, "My brother's a dumbshit. Follows me everywhere."

"When I was his age I had already run away from home, twice," Scott said. The afternoon passed, and Scott rushed Robert out the side yard when he heard the garage door open.

"You need a lift home?" the driver said. The man's expression said that it did not matter one way or another.

Robert was still standing under the tree when the truck made a second pass. The passenger door popped open, and Scott motioned to him from within. Robert sprinted to the truck and dove inside.

"If it's on your way."

"Sure it's on my way."

"I'm not allowed to have friends over," he said. "My dad's only rule. Stewart knows I'll kill him if he tells."

The driver reached a hand across to Robert. "Name's Clay," he said.

"We were halfway home when Scott said you'd kill someone if you never got to ride in this truck."

At lunchtime, it was raining and the students huddled under the eaves in clusters, leaning against the stucco walls.

"Saturday's the car wash," a girl named Julie said. She was a cheerleader.

"I'll be there," Scott said. "One way or another."

"It's a fundraiser," Julie said. "We need new uniforms."

He drove intensely, weaving in and out of traffic. He slammed on the brakes and screamed epithets with a smile.

"How old are you, Clay?" Robert said.

"How old are *you*?" Clay said.

"We're both thirteen," Robert said.

"Just double that," Clay said. "Piece a cake."

Each day, Clay would pick them up from school and drive to Scott's house.

"Scooter over here made me." Clay nudged Scott. "Said you were the funniest guy he knew."

"Naw," Robert said. "Paul," he said. "Paul Spielman's a lot funnier than me. He can do that thing with his pinky."

Clay smoked indoors, helped himself to the liquor cabinet, and made himself at home. At 4:00 each afternoon, Robert was politely asked to leave.

"Come on," Scott said. "Do the frog."

"I like jokes," Clay said.

"Robert doesn't tell jokes," Scott said. "He does voices."

Clay dropped Robert off at the corner of Fairfield and Lupine with a pat on the back and a promise to see him again.

"Why?" Robert would ask.

Clay and Scott were smiling, waiting. Robert glanced out the window. A very old woman in a white suit was slumped behind the wheel of her Buick.

Robert caught a fever. He thrashed uselessly in his bed. His mother entered his room and said that he was blessed to have a home and a family, especially a mother who cared for him. "Some mothers throw their kids out on the street," she warned.

"Hey man," Clay would say. "Scott's my best buddy. Best buddies gotta have their time together." Then he would mess Scott's blond hair.

Robert became the frog. "I want to unbutton that blouse and show grandma what a good grandson I am," he croaked. "Young or old, it don't matter to me."

"Saw you chilling in that big-ass truck," said Julie.

"Yeah, Clay and I are buddies," Scott said. "Went over to my house yesterday, watched a couple movies. Clay's into shit I never even knew existed."

Robert started a rumor at the middle school, that Scott and Clay were lovers. It spread quickly.

"It makes sense," Robert heard a lanky basketball player say as they passed each other. "It makes sense because the truck is so high, nobody can see what they do inside it."

“Don’t talk to me about that gay shit,” Scott said. He crossed his arms. “This is Robert, girls. He knows Clay too. Clay thinks he’s a funny motherfucker.”

One night, Robert woke from a bad dream, dressed, and silently crept out of his house. He headed to the Shell station.

“Clay is hot,” said another girl, Heather, who kept flinging her hair. “You think so, Scott? Would you do him?”

Robert spent his lunch hour near the tennis courts, alone. He spat into the gravel until his throat was dry. *I am a man on the lam*, he thought, but he didn’t believe it. *I am a real fucker*, he thought, and this felt more appropriate. *A fucker and a liar.*

Clay was sitting behind bulletproof glass, under a yellow light.

“You’re a comedian,” Scott would say to Robert. “Come on, be funny.”

Robert knocked on the glass. Clay smiled and put down his book.
“Robjob.” he said. “Hello, stranger.”

“You’re funny, huh?”
“Tell us a joke. Something dirty.”
“I don’t know any jokes.”
“He does voices, girls.”
“Scott’s just fucking around.”

“Nasty habit,” Clay said. He slid a pack and some matches through the night drawer. “On me. What are you doing in twenty minutes?”
“Nothing,” he said.

Robert inhaled through his nose and listened to his body. He walked to Heather, threw his arms around her, and pushed his tongue in her mouth. There was a choking sound.

“Here’s what you do. Run across the intersection, and hop the fence. Smoke yourself a couple of cigarettes and take a seat on the picnic benches. I’m off in twenty. We’ll watch the sunrise over the lake.”

“Lonely,” Robert said. It just slipped out.

“The nastiest!” Scott yelled.

The cigarette made him dizzy; he stamped it out with his shoe. He heard Clay struggle over the chain-link fence, which rattled feebly.

Robert found Scott out on the football field. He was also alone. “Hey,” Robert said.

“I guess you’ve heard the rumor,” Scott said.

They sat with their eyes to the lake. Clay wore tapered blue jeans and white sneakers.

“How’s Scott?” Robert said.

“He was moping around all last week, but he’s fine now. He’s pretty cute when he’s got something on his mind. My little buddy. . . .”

“You don’t even know half of what Clay knows,” Scott yelled. “He knows everything. I wish these fuckers could understand what I’ve given to have a friend like that. They have no idea. Friends like that don’t come cheap.”

“He’s my buddy, too,” Robert said.

“I’m no pussy,” Scott said. “Clay’s no pussy either. You’ll see.” He indicated with his hands that he wished to be left alone.

"No," Clay said, "I would say he isn't. Scott is your friend, though he might not think so now. Not your buddy. There's a difference." Clay coughed into his hand and then spat in the grass.

"Clay's weird," Robert said. "He's too old."

"A buddy is someone you take under your wing when they need help, someone that can't stand alone on their own two feet. A friend is different. Friendship is based on mutual respect. Scott respects you."

"Clay wants to get his truck washed," Scott reported. "He wants you to come."

"He's a good kid. I saw his need for guidance, and I answered it. Have you seen the condition of their house? Mom is gone. And Dad? Where is Dad? Working, golfing. They are better off now. I cook and I clean. And I listen to Scott when he's got something troubling him. That little brother of his is a real pain in the ass, though. Very demanding. Stewart is not my buddy, I can tell you that."

"ROBJOB! ROBJOB!" Clay said through the PA. "WE HAVE A DIRTY MISSION TO ACCOMPLISH. BOARD THE VEHICLE AT YOUR OWN RISK!"

Scott stopped waiting at the bus stop after school. Instead, when the bell rang, he skated off school grounds as fast as he could, to a shady spot where the red truck was waiting.

A sliver of the red sun was visible as it climbed a distant foothill.

"Do you and Scott do things together?" Robert said.

"Be more specific, Robjob."

"Husband and wife things."

Robert picked up the phone. It was Scott. "I need you to come over here as fast as you can," Scott said.

"Like picnics? TV after dinner? I don't understand." Clay was smiling wide.

"You know what I mean."

Clay shook is head.

"Fucking," Robert said. "Blowjobs."

Clay rolled down the window. "Hey, sweetie," he said. "Don't get the PA system wet, OK?" Then he rolled it up again.

"I called you from out here," Scott said, leaning against the tree in his front yard. "I'm not supposed to be out here."

"Heard about your French kiss," he said to Robert. "Maybe you'll get to finish what you started."

He put a finger to his lips. "Come with me. Be quiet. Be really quiet. I have to show you something."

"Ooooooh," Clay said. "That really was one nasty rumor that got started."

"Yeah."

"Kids have come by the station when I'm working. They throw eggs at the glass. They've even slashed the tires on my truck."

"Where's my watchdog?" he said, croaking hoarsely. "Did my watchdog abandon his post?"

"Would you ever do those kind of things?" Robert said. "The husband and wife stuff."

"Why do you ask?"

The bedroom door opened a crack, and Clay peered into the hallway. He began muttering everything Robert had said in the voice of the frog.

"If you wanted to do them with me that would be OK with me," Robert said. Clay laughed. Then he laughed again. "You remind me of myself when I was your age," he said.

"I'm not like you."

"Give it a few years and then we'll see."

"Man oh man, look at those titties! What would you give to stick your dick right in between those?" The girls smiled as they worked.

"Robert, do a voice," Scott said.

"I like to come out here before work and watch the ducks."

His arm extended toward the closed white door. "Just so you know it wasn't me he wanted," Scott said.

Robert looked at the brown water. There were no ducks—none visible, anyway.

"I'm gonna tell you a secret," Clay said, "but you can't tell anyone."

"Do you like it?"

"What?"

"The lake."

"Not really."

"Ha. Me neither."

He rolled up the window, and the girls began hosing the truck down. Then they took to it with soapy sponges.

"So," he said. "No voices?" He fixed his green eyes on Robert.

"No voices," Robert said. "Not for a while."

Murder Ballad

Can you hear me calling you? Here I am, calling you: can you hear me?

Barely, yes. Faintly. Is it really you?

Your sugar baby; your true love. Don't I sound the same?

You're a little hoarse.

Well, you sound the same.

Where are you?

Baby, you know me. You know where I am.

I'd hoped not.

You are missing out big time; the flames are so beautiful! They dance and dance into the night sky! I wish you were with me, baby, just walking the grounds. Arm in arm, and baby, too . . . I'm on a short break, actually. Just wanted to get in touch.

He gives you breaks?

The Devil's so generous, sweetie. He encourages exercise, plenty of rest. Do you want to know what he told me last night?

No.

I just couldn't sleep last night, on account of thinking of you! So I went out walking the grounds, and was kind of perusing the fence that hems us in, when I saw the Devil, stooped over with his cutters, making a hole in his own fence!

Just to torture you.

You'd think so, wouldn't you, darling? But no; he told me I could leave if I wanted to, anytime that was convenient for me. He said it's a great misunderstanding that one has to work eternally, baby. He tries telling people the truth, but they don't listen. Do you know why they don't listen?

I have to go.

They don't listen to what the Devil's telling them because they're so happy here. The warmth, the job, the sense of community. Shared purpose, shared goals.

That sounds terrible, everybody penned in together.

Well, the Devil's said some not-so-nice things about where you are.

He would.

He said that the Lord likes his creatures nice and docile, so he keeps them on a short tether. Hey, tell me, have you managed to stay young? Kept your good looks?

I'm trying not to listen to you.

Pretend to hear me anyway.

I don't know how I look. When I try and catch my reflection, say, in a pond, the only thing I ever see is the blue sky behind me.

You sound bored, baby.

Honestly, I want for nothing.

Tell me all about yourself.

I'm going to stop listening to you.

What can I do? I'm still in love. We were parted so suddenly, honey.

It was sudden.

And I leave you alone for just a little while and you forget about me?

How long has it been?

Don't know. I've been shoveling coal, pulling long hours. My hair's almost gone gray. They have mirrors here, so many mirrors, so I have proof. My face even started to wrinkle!

So you've lost your looks?

I think I'm pretty distinguished, actually. You'd still like me.

How were you able to reach me?

I'll be in touch soon.

Don't.

•

Can you hear me calling, a little clearer? Just a little bit clearer?

A little clearer, yes. I can hear you.

Tell me baby, would you take it all back?

Take what back?

All those mean things you said?

No.

I don't believe it.

I would say them again.

You're being dramatic.

It's just that it's been so long. I was planning my life without you.

Do you ever get sad, baby? I got so sad today.

I don't. Not here, I mean.

I was thinking back today, remembering how poor we were. Do you remember how little we had?

You weren't a good saver.

Not true, honey. Not true at all. We tried to make it work, but our jobs just didn't pay!

I've been meaning to ask you something.

Go ahead.

Were you really fired, or did you just quit?

Well, since it doesn't matter anymore, I'll tell you the truth. I quit, baby. I told them to shove it, that I just wasn't cut out for it.

Your upbringing spoiled you, I think.

How could I stand such a menial job? It was so degrading. For you, I can see how it might have been different. You started with nothing, so you had no standards.

I fell for you, didn't I?

Don't beat yourself up. And anyway, you did love me.

You were all I had. My mother dead and my father ailing. My sister and I working to keep the business.

You were so beautiful when you worked. Hair pinned back, sleeves rolled up, hunched over your work. I fell in love with you like that.

Just a college boy getting his kicks. Washing his clothes in the bad part of town. I see it all now, your smug tourism.

This is so unfair. I dropped out of school for you, brought myself down to you. I'm going to go.

Tell me it was worth it, at least. I don't want to think that we wasted our time.

All of it. Every moment.

That's been bothering me.

It's that doubt of yours.

What about it?

It's the only reason you can hear me.

I am happy, though.

That's all I ever wanted.

That's a lie.

Baby, all I ever wanted was for you to be happy. And also, I'm not ashamed to say it, to fuck you in the morning.

But then you quit your job, and I was stuck working mornings. And we lost that balance, which is so necessary.

Do you remember the hole in the curtain? How the sunlight would fall through it and lie along your hip?

If I don't remember it's because I was sleeping.

I was watching, baby. That's important. Remember how I would kiss your hand? Every chance I had I would kiss your hand?

Pacifying me.

Did I tell you I got my singing voice back? I sing all day long now, as I shovel. Let me sing you our ballad. You remember our ballad, don't you?

No.

One song.

I said no.

Oh, two lovers in love / They love and love and love / They love each other so much that they threaten to engulf each other / They formulate a plan in love / Arrangements are lovingly made / And with love the plan is carried out / Until everything gets fucked up because someone comes to doubt.

I remember that melody. The lyrics you've changed, of course. It's terrible.

You don't like the new verse?

Your voice twists me all up. Goodbye.

•

Can you hear me calling, louder now?

Your voice is stronger. I thought you might've taken the hint.

Listen: I was shoveling today, thinking about you. The flames were so warm on my face. They felt good. I even worked up a sweat. Then I realized something.

This should be good.

I realized that I've kind of been dominating our conversations. I want to hear more from you. Tell me what it's like there.

You really want to know?

Heaven is hard for me to visualize.

It's practically empty. I can go several hours without seeing anyone at all. We have meadows and lakes and ponds and streams and rolling green hills.

I always thought the congestion would be terrible. Do you recognize anyone? Any of our old friends?

We had no friends. You drank with those men at the bar, but they weren't our friends. I wasn't allowed to know them.

You could have come! You never asked. How was I supposed to know you cared?

That's what a husband does: he knows. Didn't you feel how damp my pillow was when you came home? I cried every night, near the end. You could never get your shoes off without waking me up.

I took off my shoes to do my part. To keep the house clean!

I kept the house clean.

You kept such a clean house. Sometimes I'd see the kitchen tile shining so bright, and I'd drop right to my knees and give it a good lick.

There are only two types of people here.

I know, honey, the righteous and the saved.

The only people here are babies or those murdered.

But you weren't murdered!

Someone decided that I was.

What about our baby, honey? The poor thing you brought with you!

We haven't crossed paths, though some have seen her. The babies move so slowly here. One day I'll meet her, I know that. It's inevitable, given the lack of time. But I'm not hurrying. She's not getting any older, and neither am I.

Have you met Jesus yet? What a treat that would be. . . .

Not yet. They say He'll arrive at such and such place at this time, but the terrain is pretty interchangeable here, so I've never caught Him. Granted, it is beautiful landscape, but after a while, a perfect lake or a perfect meadow tends to lose a little of its excitement. I do want to meet Him, though. They say He's very personable.

You think He remembers what we used to say about Him?

I don't know what you're talking about.

I'll bet you do. In the final stages, when we finally decided to go through with it. You remember, sugar.

We were so young, though. Your books gave you the saddest, ill-formed ideas. Loving you, I made myself believe them. What else could I have done? I made your beliefs mine.

Name one. You don't remember them.

Oh, that all effort was useless, that life had a cold black center, that hell cared more for the two of us than anything in the world. Do you know what the worst part was?

That they were all true?

That you took pleasure in feeding me these lies. That was the worst; that you enjoyed yourself. My time here has given me a chance to consider how you've wronged me.

Is that what you do there? Open old wounds?

It's actually quite amazing what we do here. When you arrive, your entire memory is given back to you, from the day of your birth to the day of your death.

So you've been spending time with me after all?

I guess.

I'm sorry, angel. I'm going to go.

It's been good to hear your voice.

Well, it's good to hear you say that. I know He doesn't let you lie up there. Honey, it won't be long.

•

Can you hear me calling from the canyon?

I hear you. I have some big news.

What happened, honey?

I found our daughter today.

Our baby girl? Where?

She was crawling through a meadow.

Is she pretty like her mamma?

She has your strange neck, but her eyes are all mine. She's on my hip right now.

Give her a kiss from me! Have you been missing me?

I don't know.

Were you worried when I didn't call?

I assumed you were working late.

Actually, baby, I've been on the move. I was talking with the Devil the other day; he's got such a honey tongue. He said that the only thing separating us is a canyon, that we're both on the same plane. Isn't that wild?

He tells you what you want to hear. Besides, I'm free to walk. I would have discovered it.

He also said that your good master blinds you to this. You can't see it, baby.

You have no idea what you're talking about.

Do you know what's keeping me going on my little hike? Thinking about our goodbye. You remember that place. Under those big trees?

I can't.

Do you mean you won't?

I don't know.

Do you remember tripping through the tall grass? We were gone on wine, angel. Lovers in love.

I remember the tall grass, but I never tripped. I walked tall. It was you who fell, who hit your head on that rock.

But your legs were so long and slim, darling. They tangled.

I'm nothing like that now. I practically float over the plain.

Remember those dappled shadows of the trees?

There were no shadows; the sun had fallen too far.

The dress you wore, that pretty stitching?

I've been given new clothes here.

Such a pretty gun we carried.

You were so proud of that thing.

So romantic, we were, walking under those trees in our fancy clothes.

I wish we would have picked a nicer stream to sit by. The water was so dirty.

Remember the thought we held to, angel? The one we placed before us?

Husband, wife, and child—all together. The Devil preparing three places.

We were so brave! But when I put the barrel to your hair. . . .

Everything we ever said seemed silly.

And you stopped loving me.

I screamed for you to stop, but the bullet passed through me, and I arrived here. I started walking, and haven't stopped since.

Baby, I never heard you scream! I saw your eyes get wild with fear, though, and I knew I had lost you. I just couldn't go through with it knowing I had lost you.

You were afraid.

It wasn't fear, honey, so much as hurt feelings.

You knew you were a murderer.

I was feeling so down, I cried three tears, right there. One for me, one for you, one for baby. Then I sank you in the stream and rolled a boulder onto your back, so you wouldn't rise.

Please stop.

I left you there, wondering if there was anyone out there in the world for me. I wanted to start over. To have a new family. I called your sister, but she never cared for me. I put up ads for myself. I went back on the dating scene. But no one wanted to be with me. The police barged in our house one morning, tramping all over that clean tile with their boots. I evaded them. As I was fleeing, my mind was racing, and I thought maybe—just maybe—I'd made a mistake. That maybe I hadn't lost you after all.

You'd lost me.

I returned to the trees, to the stream where I had hid you. I dredged you up, and lay down beside you. Little fish had taken your soft parts, honey, but you were still beautiful. And that's how I left the world: by your side, looking at you. Then I arrived here, and made a life for myself. Happy growing old, you know, but missing a little something. . . .

You're just a sick old man.

We all grow old here, honey, but the Devil keeps us working. Actually, I saw your father recently. A foreman in the mines, poor guy. Looks like his bones have gotten tired of propping up his skin. Pretty scary sight. But he works hard; he's appreciated down here.

I wish you would leave me alone.

Some sweet day, angel. Some sweet day I'll die again and turn to dust. But for now, there's work to be done!

Goodbye.

Honey, I'm nearly there. The canyon's steep, but I'm motivated. Dodging the bones of the others, like me, but without my agility. Where will we meet?

•

Can you hear me calling you? It should be perfectly clear.

•

On your side now. Have the wind carry your voice to me.

•

I've just met your colleagues, honey. Such a sad, pallid lot. All gone in nostalgic reverie. But they were helpful; they know how lonely it gets. They've directed me your way.

•

I see you across the stream, both of you. I'm waving from the other side. You recognize me; you do. Why would you look away? Honey angel baby sweetie darling sweetheart—my last kind words. See how baby reaches for me? It's OK, give her to me. I'll toss her up and catch her. Listen to her laugh. A laugh must be so rare in this sanctified place. Don't cry, please. You'll have a job soon, you'll be useful again. We'll have our own place, a place in the comforting flames, a little apartment. And we'll laugh together. We'll learn how. When you ask me how my day went and I ask you how your day went we'll both just laugh and laugh and laugh until the flesh falls from our bones and we'll be two skeletons in love.

Come on, open your eyes and see me.

Last Seen

A mother and her son sit at their kitchen table. They are ruined people, both in appearance and spirit. Also, they are not financially well-off.

There was, and still might be, a brother to the son, a son to the mother. He disappeared not long ago, took the dog for a walk one bright Saturday and never came back.

We sympathize. We really do. So would he. Pity is easy for us; it's empathy that we find difficult. But we'll give it a try. We give all people one or two or possibly three chances.

It's late afternoon. The light is ugly and yellow and violating the darkness as it streams through the blinds. At least that's the mother's opinion. Everything has become awful to her: the light, the dark, the modest house in which they live, the people they encounter on a daily basis. Except of course her son, whom she still loves.

The son has not yet reached his mother's stage of evacuation. But, to be fair, though young, he already has some seedling of hatred growing in his heart. He is only nine, but has the face of an old man. It has been a difficult three months. The son doesn't know this yet, but he will have to learn to live with his face. He believes he will shed it in adulthood. He is so sweet and wrong.

They, the mother and son, channel different frequencies of pain. Neither knows exactly what the other is feeling. This is a condition invented long ago by a pervert. To each his own private horror, the pervert says. Grief will be unending and barely endurable. Lay all your troubles on you know who.

It seems unrealistic that one family should suffer so much, we think. Awful statistics, we say, random accidents. (A plan, he says. A developing plan.)

There are some woods near the house, a square mile at the end of the street. Bring on the deforested future, we say. Less places to get lost. What is a child's safety to a little lost wood?

The son has a notebook, on which he's written the facts of the case. He doesn't fully understand what he's written. He just writes what he hears, what he reads or sees on television. His mother stares blankly, angrily at the window and the light seeping through it.

I want to look for him, says the son.

Why? says the mother.

We've been letting other people look.

They have been over this many times. The son still believes that his brother can be found.

Why don't we look for him?

Where would we look?

The woods, says the son.

We've looked in the woods.

Somewhere else, then.

The world is too large.

Why do you want to forget him?

I can't forget him.

The mother is right, of course. Oh, that we could forget everything, we say.

Why don't you care? says the son.

But I do, says the mother. I'm trying to accept his absence. I hope you can, too.

But he's not gone. He's missing.

Really? Do you really believe that?

Come look for him with me, says the son.

The mother turns her face toward him. Her expression is haggard, furious. Think for a moment, she says. What do we know?

About what?

What are the facts?

Why? says the son. He looks at his mother with his poor hopeful face.

I'll help you if you answer me, she says.

OK.

Where was he last seen?

He was last seen at the trailhead.

By whom?

He was last seen by an elderly couple at the trailhead.

Our neighbors. Who are decrepit cunts.

Why would you call them that?

Tell me what they saw.

They saw him talking to a gray-haired man in a gray truck.

And?

They took down the license plate and walked away.

Decrepit cunts.

Why would you call them that?

A decrepit cunt has a keen sense of danger but not the courage to locate the source of the danger, for they are too decrepit. Hence the taking down of the license plate without actually intervening.

So he was last seen by our neighbors, an elderly couple, who are a pair of decrepit cunts.

Yes. Read me what else you have.

Our dog was found in the woods, walking alone without a leash.

And what did we do with the dog?

We put it to sleep.

And why did we do that?

Because it was a reminder of my brother.
Yes. What else do you have there?
The police were able to find the truck, because of our neighbors.
What did they find in the truck?
They found two things, says the son.
Which were?
They found a dog leash.
And whose dog did the leash belong to?
Ours.
And where is our dog?
In the ground.
Good. What else did they find?
They found something that wasn't there.
What was it?
They found that the seatbelt had been cut out.

Good. And what did police find in the dumpster behind the supermarket?

They found the seatbelt that had been cut out.
And what was special about the seatbelt?
It was soaked with blood.
Did it match your brother's blood type?
Yes.
How does this make you feel?
Scared. How does it make you feel?
Angry.
Why not scared?
I'm not scared of anything. What did the police not find?
The gray-haired man and my brother.
And why haven't they found your brother?
Because they haven't found the gray-haired man yet.
And why haven't they found the gray-haired man?
Because the police are limited?
Yes. Any other reason?
Because the gray-haired man is wily.

Yes. How does this make you feel?
Angry. Stop asking me questions.
Why?
You're making me scared.
OK.
Do you remember your sister?
Yes.
What happened to her?
She was killed by a car.
And what happened to the perpetrator?
He went to jail.
Do you remember your father?
Yes.
And what happened to him?
He died of cancer.
And what happened to the cancer?
It died with him.
Good. Do you see how these things happen?
Yes.
Do you believe your brother is dead?
No.
Why not?
Because he is still missing.
But the facts.
I know.
Do you believe that the gray-haired man is guilty?
Yes.
And what has happened to him?
Nothing.
What do we need to do?
Find my brother.
No, says the mother. What do we need to do?
I don't know.
Who do we need to find?

The gray-haired man.

Yes. Why?

I don't know.

Will he bring your brother back?

No.

Why do we need to find the gray-haired man?

Because he can tell us what he knows.

Good. But will what he knows bring your brother back?

No.

Why?

Because my brother is probably dead.

Good. Then why would we care to listen to the gray-haired man?

I don't know.

Because the gray-haired man will have interesting things to say.

Since when do we care about hearing interesting things?

We are starting today.

I don't want to.

Do we have anything else to look forward to?

Why do you keep reminding me that my brother is dead?

Because grief has made me strange.

Me too.

I'm sorry.

Are you making an excuse?

Yes. Is it a good one?

Yes.

She takes her son's head in her hands and kisses him. Do you know why I love you?

Because I'm your last one?

No.

Why then?

Because you will never die.

I hope so.

Do you still want to look for your brother?

Yes.

Get your coat, then.

We might have made a mistake. The world is too big and full of life to dwell here, we think. Broad parody, we shout. They don't resemble anyone we know. The mother? Sadism drives her. The son? Delusional, traumatized. Write him off. Write them both off, we say. In fact, write off the house, the neighborhood, the neighbors, the woods, the whole town, everyone is clearly complicit.

Here is a scene we would much prefer: a mother and her son sit at the breakfast table. The mother serves the son pancakes, the son eats them with gratitude. The son is getting ready for school, the mother speaks to him of the coming day. (Have compassion, he would say. Honor those beneath you with your attention. The mother is the very picture of endurance, the son innocent, incorruptible.) Fine, we say. Just get them out of the house, into the sunlight, the fresh air. Please just get them out of the house!

The mother and son begin to look. They leave the house, the mother closing the door behind them. Outside: autumn and its acute sadness. Piles of fallen leaves. The air is cold, beautiful to breathe in.

The mother takes her son's hand. They don't speak, making their way to the woods. This would be an appropriate time to pull away, we think. To be left with this image. Two wretched people strengthened only by each other. But we are feeling better outside.

We don't dare search their thoughts, yet we stay with them. Our own motivation escapes us, sometimes.

The mother and son are at the trailhead now, looking. They enter the woods, the pine trees tall and teetering slightly in the wind. The son points to places off the trail, a hollow trunk, a branch, the dirty stream, and they search them all. They wind their way through the square mile, sometimes on the path, sometimes off, until both believe that they've exhausted every hiding place.

When they reach the trailhead, the mother stops and squeezes her son's hand.

Are you satisfied? says the mother.

Yes, says the son.

Did you see the gray-haired man?

No. Did you?

Yes.

Where was he?

He was high up in a tree.

What was he doing?

Looking.

Did he see you?

Yes, says the mother.

What did he do?

He regarded me.

What did you do?

I regarded him.

Should we tell anyone?

No.

Why not?

He's not going to hurt us.

How do you know?

Because you can't hurt someone when you are high up in a tree.

Shouldn't he be punished?

I don't know.

Why didn't you tell me?

I didn't want you to be scared.

I wouldn't have been scared.

Do you want to see him now?

No, says the son. Did you see my brother?

No. Did you?

Yes.

Where was he?

He was high up in a tree.
Did he see you?
No.
I'm sorry. What was he doing?
I don't know.
Was he dead?
Yes.
Why didn't you tell me?
I didn't want you to be angry.
I wouldn't have been angry.
Do you want to see him now?
No.
Why not? says the son.
I remember him alive, says the mother. I would like to keep it that way.
Do you want to go home?
Yes.
Good.

We walk them to their door, but only out of courtesy. At last the sun has fallen, the putrid light finally gone. The neighborhood is dark, the woods darker. Well, the mother and son are clearly deranged beyond help. And the killer? The victim? High up in trees! We've seen everything. Or enough, at least. Enough to recall, later, if necessary. It was our mistake. Yes, we've made the mistake. We could have stayed at home, on the other side of town. We have families there: healthy ones. We lead reasonably healthy lives. We have no business getting carried away. (He will call us weak-stomached, infantile, rational, graceless.) Let him. Let him threaten us vaguely. Pervert. Decrepit cunt. We'll see, we'll see. Let them tell it themselves, we say:

good morning son good morning mother did you sleep well yes and you yes I made you some pancakes i would love some come sit down i will are you still satisfied yes are you yes do you know why i love you because i will live forever yes and because you are my last one will you live forever yes I will do you miss the rest of them yes every one of them do you every one of them but we are getting along yes we are getting along will you answer the door yes I will hello sit down please sit down please we are listening yes we are listening what do you have to say please tell us what you have to say you don't need to apologize or even explain just tell us what you have to say.

I Shall Not Be Moved

I will not be separated from the city I love. Here I have found, if not complete acceptance of who I am, an environment in which I am able to exploit the odd dimensions of my body to achieve something resembling a normal life.

My lover and I have worked out our routine: from Monday to Saturday of every week, he walks me, just as he does now, to the Golden Lantern before continuing on to work. While he works, I sit on the bar and drink with my friends. At five in the evening he drops by to pick me up, ordering a soda and catching up on what he has missed. Then we walk back home, and I lightly fuck my lover until I climax or become too tired to continue.

Sundays, on the other hand, are relaxing days. My lover goes to church, and I sleep all day long. I do not touch a drop out of consideration for his religious beliefs, though that is perhaps the only concession I will make for him.

I am, admittedly, a bit stubborn. But beyond that, the stress from evacuating this city would put an unnecessary strain on my heart, which is already and, I should say, naturally, a bit overworked. My lover does not know this, and I don't want to worry him with something he cannot alter. For all his supposed interest in little people, though, he has no idea of the very real medical problems we daily face.

It is a lovely, slightly overcast Saturday morning, and the heat is as it always is in August: wet and persistent. I am in my usual leather, my lover's favorite. My lover and I live in a shotgun in the Marigny, so our walk is an easy stroll west on Royal Street into the French Quarter. Were it any other day, the street would be full of sweet, silly men, meticulously cleaning up behind their tiny dogs. Today, however, there are only a few, but they're busy packing their belongings into their cars, with grim, distracted looks on their faces. I would say that the mood is slightly anxious, were I not several gin and tonics into my morning, and therefore immune to such sensitivities.

When we reach the Golden Lantern, my lover kisses my cheek and hands me a hundred dollar bill. It is an unusually high sum.

"I want you to get whatever you want," he says. "I want you to get as drunk as you possibly can."

"So that you can kidnap me and drag me to Houston?" I ask.

"Oh, Derrin," he says, "you've figured out my plan."

"Yes, I have," I say, "and that is why I will only drink soda until you return."

"If you stay sober today," he says, "I won't ask you to evacuate ever again. But only if you stay sober. If not, I'll ask you when I return, I'll ask you as we walk home, I'll ask you long into the night and all of next day, when landfall is predicted."

"Promise me something," I say, buttoning my leather vest with an important air, "that if we do stay, and we find ourselves in the situation where we are both hungry, and surrounded by water, with no help in sight, I want you to promise that you will eat me to survive."

"Don't joke about that," he says.

"Promise me. "

"I won't."

"Then at least promise me that after I am dead, and you have thoughtfully buried me, that you will enlist the services of a woman to have your child, and once the child is born you will name him Derrin, or Derrina, after me, after the little man you once knew." I nibble at my lover's palm.

"I won't eat you. I don't want children either."

"But dear," I say, "don't you know that if the city is destroyed, and our house is underwater, and the Golden Lantern is closed indefinitely, and you are going hungry right before my very eyes, don't you know that I would want you to eat me?"

"I'll see you after a while," he says. I give him my empty cup to throw away.

The Golden Lantern is a long, rectangular room, smoky and intimate and not for the faint of heart. Occasionally a curious tourist will poke a head into the bar and, finding the assortment of tawdry queens and hustlers not exactly what he or she had in mind, quickly run in the direction of Bourbon Street, where the straight and vacant dwell. Today it is very quiet; there are only two people in the place: Jimmy, who tends bar, and a handsome young boy I do not know.

"Hey, little daddy," says Jimmy. He comes to my side and lifts me up on the counter, where there is always a space cleared for me to sit. Jimmy is in his seventies and speaks through a voice box in his throat, and he is by far the most courteous person I know. I believe he beat his cancer simply because he never thought death might be required of him.

He pours me a gin and tonic in a plastic cup and sets it in the crook of my arm. "I have a reward waiting for me if I stay sober," I say.

"What might that be?"

I take a long swallow of the gin. "He says that if I keep to the soda today, he won't ask me to evacuate."

Jimmy points to my drink. "Do you want me to get rid of that for you, sweetie?"

"Absolutely not. I can pull myself together in time. You're staying, are you not?"

Jimmy does not hesitate before depressing the button on his voice box. "Yes, indeed," he says.

"I wish you would speak to my lover. His mind is all but made up."

I lay the large bill on the counter next to me. Jimmy looks imploringly at me. "It's from him," I say. "Let me buy you a drink. And the handsome young man over there, buy him one, too."

The young man can be no older than seventeen. He possesses the longest eyelashes I have ever seen. To my delight, the blue T-shirt he is wearing has the quite original phrase *dairy master* printed across the chest. I notice that he is scribbling furiously with a pen on several napkins.

"Little dear," I say. "Young man." He glances up from his work.

"What?" he says. "What do you want?" I do believe he's trying to sound tough.

"I want to know what you'd like to drink."

"I don't fuck for just a drink," he says.

"And I don't buy drinks for handsome young men in the hopes of fucking them," I say. "It'll be enough just watching you enjoy something."

Jimmy reassures the young man with a gentle nod of his head.

"Red Bull and vodka," the young man says. Ah, the youth and their cheap thrills!

"What are you writing?" I ask.

"Just a little poetry," he says.

"Will you share some with us?"

"You'll laugh."

"We will not. Please, immerse us in beauty."

"All right," he says. "Can I have the drink first?"

Jimmy pours the young man his request. The young man takes it down, and is revived.

"This is called, 'Young, Scared, Happy.'"

"It sounds wonderful," I say. "Is it autobiographical?"

"I don't know," he says. "I'm going to start now."

"Wonderful," I say.

"I dance in the dark,
Without a stage.
I twirl in sexual revolution,
Without protection.
My heart is exposed,
My heels dug in.
And the people protest,
They rage,
They stand erect.
Yet I shall not be moved.
I shall not be moved."

Jimmy and I applaud. It is a shame that the city of New Orleans should lavish so much attention on its music, when there is clearly an equally vital poetry scene. I, for one, have always wanted to put my complex feelings into lines. I ask the young man if he's staying for the storm.

"I moved here two weeks ago," he says. "I don't know what to do. The news is scaring me, though. What are you doing?"

"I don't want to leave," I say, "but my lover insists that we go. I am in a bit of a bind."

"More drinks, then," Jimmy says.

We all three pleasantly fill the time. There is small talk about business, about drama from the previous night, about the largest we have ever taken. I am quickly catapulting to a place beyond inebriated. I check the clock on the wall, and find that it's a little past one in the afternoon. All three of us have graduated to taking shots, still on the hundred dollars my lover gave me.

"What could we do to commemorate this day?" Jimmy asks.

The young man has a secretive thought in response to Jimmy's question, and he whispers it in his ear. Jimmy smiles naughtily.

"Well, little daddy," Jimmy says, "Are these the last days?"

"We would be the last to know," I say. "Can you please help me down?"

Jimmy lifts me from the counter to the floor. I walk toward the bathroom in the back of the bar. If there is one aspect of the Golden Lantern that stands to be criticized, it is the lack of a sanitary place to relieve oneself. A small quibble, but the urinal is practically mossy. I utilize it anyway.

I am thinking of my lover, I am drunk and thinking longingly of my lover. I didn't love him at first, of course, but he paid for my meals and let me stay for free in his home, as long as I fulfilled a certain duty at the end of the night. I was happy to agree to this, though I found him rather cloying and unimaginative. Over time, however, and I think it truly mysterious how these things happen, I came to see him not as my benefactor, but rather the person I was destined to love, and to test his own attachment to me, I approached him one night, and asked him how he would feel about my leaving. He admitted, with tears filling his eyes, to falling in love with me. He had not meant to, he said, but he could do nothing about it, and therefore offered me anything I wanted as long as I stayed. Sensing my opportunity, I chose the Golden Lantern six days out of the week. I think of my lover as he must be this moment, meticulously nailing plywood to his office windows. I wish he was with me, that he loved to drink as much as I.

The bar is as dark as a mausoleum as I leave the restroom. I keep the bathroom light on just to understand what is what. Someone has closed the door of the bar and lowered the blinds. I can, however, make out what is happening. The young man sits nude, on the bar counter, as Jimmy sits on a barstool, fellating him. I want to look away, but I am too intoxicated not to be interested. The young man notices me.

"I've never had a dwarf before," he says.

"Oh no?" I ask.

"I've also never had a man that couldn't talk through his mouth before, either. It's a day of firsts for me."

Jimmy presses his finger to his throat. "Derrin, he says, "give me a hand with this horse."

I have forced the fluid from a thousand members in this bar in all my years here, so this is not a shocking invitation. I am aroused within my leather pants, and I think again of my lover. I have a lover who accepts my many whims and even encourages them, who knows for a fact that I have engaged in lewd conduct in this bar and has hidden his jealousy and contented himself with the fact that, at the end of the day, I am his. I see him again, boarding up his office, preparing his mind to leave the place that he too loves. At this moment I want only him, long to be deep inside only him.

"Three's company," says Jimmy.

I am only a man, though, at the end of the day, but I do believe that certain boundaries should be set. I believe it is the Lord of scripture who says that one should be either hot or cold, to exist nowhere in the middle, but I am afraid that the man who wrote that did not spend one moment in the world that he created. It is, in fact, very advantageous to find a compromise between extremes.

I decide to stand beside Jimmy as he pleasures the young man, and am happy to simply watch. I furrow my brow and form my mouth into an o. I make low sounds in my throat. Both Jimmy and the young man are in ecstasy. The young man has reached a point of drunkenness in which he has forgotten the aged face applying suction to him, and Jimmy is thrilled to be making a boy fifty years his junior lose control. Let the storm come now, I think, let this be their eternal pose. I encourage the young man to ejaculate onto my chest, which he does with all the vigor and strength of his age. He slips from the bar and dresses. Jimmy hands me a fresh bar towel for cleanup, then raises the blinds and opens the door of the Golden Lantern. The clock tells me it is now just after two.

I take my remaining money and walk down the street to Verti-Mart, where I purchase a gallon of water, a chicken salad sandwich, and a tin of breath mints. While in line, I notice a ribbon of jissom on my leather vest, just above the breast pocket. Sweet remembrances. I wipe off the souvenir with a complimentary napkin from the deli. The clerk carries my purchases back with me to the Golden Lantern.

When I return to the bar, there are at least five more men seated at the stools, and Jimmy is listening intently as they converse. The young man sits at the far end of the bar, alone, scribbling his beautiful poems on napkins. A man I recognize but cannot name lifts me to my place on the counter. He feeds me my sandwich and lifts the container of water to my lips, stroking my hair. An angel.

It seems that since I've been gone, a mandatory evacuation has been ordered, and even if the storm were to drop to a category three, catastrophic flooding is likely. I imagine my lover and me on the rooftop of our little shotgun, the water rising all around, the music from an invisible orchestra swelling dramatically. Our neighbors paddle by in boats, waving to us, wishing us well. Some offer us a seat, but we say no, we will not leave our home, not until we are forced to swim. Just as the water rises to our necks, when my lover and I are standing, but for our heads, fully underwater on our rooftop, we kiss, and as we do, the waters recede, defeated by the power of love.

The patrons are chatty, frightened and chatty. Promises are made, vows are forged. Meet me here at x time, my friend has a generator, and he has a place for you to sleep, we live on the highest ground in the city, yes we have a few weapons, he's comfortable with me bringing people home, we'll paddle through the city, we will be the royalty of the new Atlantis, no, the cats will be safe, we'll store them in the attic, I won't leave and neither should you.

Why should it be that this should ever end? I wonder. These people have found this place, they have traveled across the entire world to find this place, the place that they have searched for their entire lives. What kind of prude, I wonder, would bring his fist down and smash it?

•

My lover arrives at four in the Mercedes; I watch him, now completely sober, from my perch on the counter. The urgency of his mission requires that he park on the curb. I realize with horror that the sedan is packed full of our belongings.

He is, of course, in quite a state. His shirt is unbuttoned at the top, his tie has fallen. He is sweating terribly, entering the bar. "Derrin," he says, "We need to go."

I point to the nearly empty jug of water. "Don't you have something to not ask me?"

"There isn't time," he says. He lifts me to the floor.

"So we are staying. Wonderful!" I shout.

"We can't stay, baby."

"You promised me that if I was in my right mind, you wouldn't ask me to leave. Here I am, in my right mind."

"I'm sorry. We need to go."

"What has happened?" I ask.

My lover thinks for a moment. He is troubled by everything. He is sensitive to every living thing at every moment. It is why I love him. This realization does not dampen my fury at being taken advantage of, however. "I couldn't live if something happened to you," he says.

"What made you suddenly disregard our agreement?"

"For some reason," he says, "I can't stop imagining the neighborhood under water, and your body floating in it."

"But don't you understand that if I were floating in the flood, the sight of our neighborhood, preserved for all time, would make me happy? I don't want to leave. What will all these boys do?"

"They will be all right. I hope the Lord will keep them safe."

"I don't understand why you think the Lord would discriminate in who He saves and who He does not. I would think that, you being a believer, and me being at least a partial acknowledger, that we would stand a fairly good chance."

"We live a life of sin," my lover says. "You know it, Derrin. We need to look out for ourselves."

My lover and his Catholic guilt! I feel an erection stirring. He becomes a fearful altar boy before my eyes. Still, I feel the need to hold my ground, though I don't know yet how to go about this.

"I'm going to the restroom," I say. I hand him the remaining three dollars of the hundred he gave me. "Why don't you order a soda and say hello to Jimmy?"

I once again make my way toward the back of the bar. Instead of entering the restroom, I slip into the shadowy part of the hallway and lean my back against the wall. From here I can see everything, all patrons, though they would have to look hard to see me. I watch my lover as he makes his way to the bar. There are several open seats, but he chooses the one next to the young poet, who sizes my lover up, wearing a face at once pensive and passionate, if such things are possible, and it is only after Jimmy has poured my lover a drink that my lover finally notices the young man's efforts. He engages the young man in polite conversation, and it is obvious, by my lover's body language, that he is quite attracted to the young man. My lover puts two fingers to his own lips when he is taken with something, as he does now.

I am not jealous. My lover is a born caregiver, above anything, and if there was ever someone who exuded fragility, albeit knowingly, it's this young man. Watching my lover now as he momentarily puts all of his fears and worries aside so as to share a pleasant moment with the young man, I find it impossible to stay angry with my lover. His manners are absolutely impeccable. I walk to him, and, pulling on his sleeve, I ask that he accompany me outside. He thanks the young man for the conversation and follows me out.

"I will go with you on one condition," I say, leaning against the beautiful sedan.

"Tell it to me," my lover says.

"That we will take one of these people with us."

"There isn't room in the car, Derrin."

"Throw out my possessions, then." I am not sure I completely mean this.

"Why do you care, baby?"

I lift one of my arms in the air magnanimously. "I care if for no other reason than you attempted to take advantage of me," I say, "and since you decided to go back on your word, I feel that I have the right to request just about anything I want. Therefore, if this storm is going to be as deadly as you say, I would like to save the life of someone else."

He smiles. "Who would you like to bring?" he graciously asks.

I walk into the bar, to the young man, and tug on the sleeve of his shirt.

"I am offering you a free ride to Houston," I say.

"I can't afford a hotel," he says.

"My lover is a lawyer," I say. "He has promised to take care of everything. I suggest you go home and pack a bag."

"I don't have a bag," he says.

"The car is waiting outside, then," I say.

I tell my lover of our new passenger, and he clears space in the back seat for the young man. Just as he finishes, I inform my lover that I will be riding in the back with the young man. "You are an evil one, Derrin," my lover says, holding back a smile. He picks me up and carries me into the bar, and we say our goodbyes. I kiss Jimmy on his precious lips.

We drive, up to our ears in all that we own, down Royal, up Conti to North Rampart, and North Rampart to Canal. I look at my lover's face in the rearview mirror. He listens to the radio, as if it held a kind of secret, cursing sweetly, taking the three of us to the freeway. The young man has brought with him his pen and a stack of napkins. He is already composing a new poem. When he finishes, he hands it to me, and I read it aloud. It is called "Three Strangers":

> "A man met another man, and formed the bond of love.
> Then they met another man, and formed the bond of friendship.

A hurricane makes them both lovers and friends.
In Houston wait the loving arms of Mother.
All lovers and friends await the loving arms of Mother."

My lover and I applaud. We are gridlocked in bumper-to-bumper traffic on Interstate 10. Seeing the faces of the others, I begin to feel a little better, knowing we are not the only ones fleeing. The young man passes me a napkin, and presses the pen into my palm.

"I cannot," I say. "My condition prevents me."

He takes them back, compassionately.

"I will tell you one instead," I say.

Acknowledgments

Without any reservations, I hereby thank the following people: Mom and Dad, Elizabeth and Patrick, Michael Martone, Kate Bernheimer, Rikki Ducornet, Bradford Morrow, Christopher Chambers, and Francine Prose.

These people also deserve something for their pains: Leah James, Laurence Ross, Katie Thompson, Earl McNair, Adam Panitch, Kate Lorenz, Adam Weinstein, Steve Kowalski, Nic De Dominic, Ryan Joe, Erik Wennermark, Cherie Weaver, and Friedrich Kerksieck.

Christopher Hellwig should get some credit too, I suppose—he line-edited the entire manuscript *for nothing*.

Stories from this collection have appeared in: *Conjunctions*—"The New Year"; *Indiana Review*—"Something in My Eye"; *New Orleans Review*—"The Vengeful Men"; *Denver Quarterly*—"The Fast Meal"; *Short Fiction*—"Repenting" and "Murder Ballad"; *Santa Monica Review*—"If We Should Ever Meet"; and *Fawlt*—"The Buddy." "The Lonesome Vehicle" originally appeared as part of the chapbook *Abandoned Tales* (Small Fires Press), and "Last Seen" first surfaced in *30 Under 30* (Starcherone Books).

Laura Schill

MICHAEL JEFFREY LEE lives in New Orleans, Louisiana, where he earns his living as a typist, a waiter, and a nightclub singer. A frequent contributor to *Conjunctions*, he is also an Associate Fiction Editor at the *New Orleans Review*. He is at work on a novel.

Sarabande Books thanks you for the purchase of this book; we do hope you enjoy it! Founded in 1994 as an independent, nonprofit, literary press, Sarabande publishes poetry, short fiction, and literary nonfiction—genres increasingly neglected by commercial publishers. We are committed to producing beautiful, lasting editions that honor exceptional writing, and to keeping those books in print. If you're interested in further reading, take a moment to browse our website, www.sarabandebooks.org. There you'll find information about other titles; opportunities to contribute to the Sarabande mission; and an abundance of supporting materials including audio, video, a lively blog, and our Sarabande in Education program.